From the Author of
When Gucci Came First
And to you, Homeboy, I say "Thanks!"
KJ Three Six Five (The Diary)
&
Man Unnecessary

WildChild Press presents…

4 Miles to Freedom

No part of this publication may be reproduced, stored in a retrieval system, or transmitted, in any form by any means, electronic, mechanical, photocopying, recording, or otherwise, without the express written permission of the author.

4 Miles to Freedom - Written by: Mia Williamson
WildChild Press - Montclair, NJ 07042
©Copyright 2007 Mia Williamson
All rights reserved.
ISBN: 0-975-3082-7-0

Although this book is based on real life situations and circumstances, its contents are fiction. This book contains strong language and is not intended for minors. Any resemblance to any persons, places or things is purely coincidental and should be regarded as such.

Written by: Mia R. Williamson

Known by these works as

"Kalico Jones"

October 2008

WildChild Press

Printed in U.S.A.

Dear Reader:

It's been a long journey, hasn't it? I want to take this time to once again thank you for having my back! This is the third and final installment of the Kalico Jones trilogy, but by no means is this my last book. I have many things left of my life's "to do" list.

Again, thank you for your support and letters, and emails and calls – hahaha, yes, I get calls too! :)

"May God grant you everything you wish for during your quiet time with Him."

Enjoy your read!

Kj.

I wanted to do something NO other author has done. I asked my Mypace friends to send me something to add to the front of this book. Comments / Critiques / Well wishes, etc. I love my MySpace friends and they can tell you that! Here's to them:

Hey Mia this is well you know who... but the Mia i know as my friend and a girl i totally did not have a clue about till i read When Gucci Came First, the book was shocking if i may say so myself and you hung wit my girlfriend for years, so was she involved in any shenanigans? Just asking' man, but at the same time you was always a good girl and a good friend. Ya Brother Aaron A.D. Duncan - 7&3, 8th and 5th holla love ya Mia

THIS IS SAMSPADE, SLAVE NAME JERALD MURPHY BIRTHDAY 10/10/ 1965. I LIKE THE WAY YOU CHEER ME UP AND BUILD ME UP. YOU ARE MY MYSPACE LIL SIS AND I LOVE YOU FOR THAT. MAY ALLAH FAVOR YOUR UNDERTAKINGS.

Kalico Jones is one of the realest people that I've never met. Over the past months as I have gotten to know her through her writings in cyber space, I've come to know someone that is true to her convictions. Her writing is powerful. Shani Greene-Dowdell - Opelika, AL (and she's an author too...Google her!)

Mia, I have always admired your Voice to speak through your writing or any outlet you've had. Over the years I've seen you channel positive energy regardless of the trails being constructive implementing your talent to express your point of view or experiences. I commend you for your tenacity and endurance. Keep up the good work. Bill Blass - Us2g Yonkers, N.Y (B. Blass...I love him – Google him, he's rapping and has a great program for kids!)

Kalico your realness makes me feel like I've known you forever and a day. You didn't know me from anybody but whenever I needed help you never hesitated to be one of the first ones there. I'm blessed to have the friend that I have in you. The only thing left to say now is I LOVE YOU KALICOOOOOO!!!! Hollywood - Ft. Washington, Maryland

I know I am going into ya book lol THERE AINT MANY CHARACTERS LIKE ME alive or dead real or made up lmao So when you profile a bruh make sure u capture the real essence of CHK DA ORIG lol – Philadelphia, PA

Mia,I must say that your friendship is very valuable to Me. I remember when I first met you, you embraced me and really made me feel good about what I do and the things I write and your kindness is something I'll always be grateful for. Author Jessica A. Robinson Youngstown, Ohio

Since day one I knew you were the truth. I'm 100% feeling your realness, your thoughtfulness, your bluntness, your sincerity, your determination, your brains & beauty all wrapped up in one creative package. Keep doing your thing. I wish nothing but the best for the best. Nomadik ENT. Holding you down mami. Love, BANG HUSKY76 PlugZone DETROIT, MICHIGAN

STAY FOCUSED SISTA & GOOD LUCK WITH YOUR BOOK DEAL! IT MAKES THIS BROTHER FEEL GOOD 2 SEE ANOTHER STRONG BLACK WOMAN ACHIEVE HER GOALS! YOU ARE A GOOD EXAMPLE FOR THESE LOST YOUNG SISTAS... WHO GOT DA GAME ASS BACKWARDS! HEALTH - WEALTH - & CONTINUED SUCCESS 2 YOU & YOUR MOVEMENT!!! ;0) MY NAME IS DOUGLAS SMALL & I'M FROM MT.VERNON NY! (914) WESTCHEDDAR!!! KEEP ON RISING 2 DA TOP MISS JONES...CAUSE YOU'RE ALMOST THERE BABEZ!

When I first met you, you welcomed me with open arms. Since then you have always kept in touch with me through comments and your stimulating blogs. I have learned a lot about myself through your blogs and it has help me with many issues in my life. It is an honor to have you as my friend and I hope we remain friends for ever. Love James Martinez - Charlotte NC

In loving Memory of
The "OLD" me

To my daughter, Ivana
You were truly meant to be

The loves of my life for holding down my daughter:

Robert B., Mel B. "Rich", Kevin H, Brandon M, Canada, Boo and the entire 3D Barber shop in Montclair who always show my daughter love, especially when she's selling books, or lotion or those Girl Scout cookies – y'all are the BEST! Brother Mahir for always being nice. Always saying "Hey Sis, how's your daughter" when he sees me. Dre for letting us come hang out for our "after the pool" food (Lol. She can eat, cant she?) Tony (good looking out with the dog), Hev (I'm still waiting for my car), My brothers Joey and Charlie and the FIRST wives club (T and L), Sha and Kiyah (and their son J – I love y'all), Shayna (You do come through when I need you), and of course, my mother, father and last, but most certainly NOT least... My step mother Karen, Brothers Josh and Dre...all my blood sisters and brothers of whom I would list, but I would probably misspell someone's name.

We thank you for everything. We are grateful to you and blessed to have such a good group of people and very positive male role models in our lives. We love each of you tremendously.

Resemblance to any person(s), place(s) or thing(s) is purely coincidental and should be regarded as such a.k.a "The disclaimer."

The Final Installment of the Kalico Jones Trilogy
4 MILES TO FREEDOM

4 Miles to Freedom

The Final installment of the Kalico Jones Trilogy

4 Miles to Freedom

OH NO SHE DIDN'T!

Yelling in the background...

"Tell Kalico not to call here again, we don't want to get involved, whatever is going on between her and homeboy is none of our business, hang up on her ass right now Rich!"

I was on the phone with one of homeboy's cousins, asking him for a number. During our talk, I told him how homeboy hadn't seen his daughter in over one year and was behind in child support. I was only calling to ask for his assistance...to help me help my daughter. We had been in and out of emergency rooms due to what was thought to be Sickle Cell, the doctors needed homeboy's medical history.

I didn't know who else to turn to.

I could not believe Rich's wife, girlfriend or whatever she goes by these days after having just had her third kid by this, another SO-CALLED family member...she was yelling, cursing and did she call me a bitch?

Ha...that was easy for her to do, as I was in New Jersey and her ass was in Mt. Vernon. Yeah, I will be that bitch, and maybe homeboy is a looser, but for the most part and other than that...WE – me and my daughter are just fine.

"Richard, why is Adrianne yelling like that in the background? What did I do to her?" as I was utterly confused by her behavior.

"KJ, she does not want you to call here any more. We all know homeboy is fucking up, but there is nothing we can do about it. That's for you two to work out."

The Final installment of the Kalico Jones Trilogy

4 Miles to Freedom

"Are you serious? So you're not going to give me his telephone number?"

"No"

"But its Sickle Cell Richard...(took a deep breath) can you please get in contact with him and just give him the number to the hospital? Please?"

(more yelling in the background by Adrianne) "Tell her no...we are not getting involved! I told you to hang up!"

I pleaded with Richard to please just pass along the number to homeboy, and as soon as he agreed, his "whatever" got on the phone and said, "Take care of your own business bitch!" and hung up.

WOW, can you believe that shit? This ingrate just hung up on me. She has three children, so it's hard for me to digest the fact that as a mother herself, she showed no compassion for my daughter. Wow.

I called back and let the phone ring. No one picked up.

Good. I will just leave a voice message.

"Hello this is Kj, my apologies for impeding upon your privacy with my issue, clearly this is something that does not involve you, but there is a child in the hospital and this is urgent. I just need to contact homeboy. The doctors are requesting blood work and a possible bone marrow sample from him. They are in need of his family's medical history. We are at Mountainside Hospital in Montclair, NJ should you wish to pass along this message." I left the telephone number to the hospital, my cell number, my job number and my mother's information as well...

I deleted Quick's cell phone number after that.

NO ONE got back to us. NO ONE called the hospital.

I even called homeboy's job.

4 Miles to Freedom

And ...NOTHING.

Eighteen tests for all sorts of shit and six days later, my daughter was released from the hospital with a clean bill of health.

Thank GOD.

Notice how I do not capitalize his name. There is no respect there and so I refuse to do it. So don't worry yourself with that...Just wanted to get that out of the way in the beginning. At any rate, life goes on.

AFTER THE HEALTH SCARE

After the health scare it was back to business and life as usual. My daughter continued to excel in school and I continued to excel professionally. I landed a wonderful job at a prestigious university and my daughter, well she landed a spot on the A honor roll and was being considered for the gifted and talented program for the next school year. Its been about 14 months since we've seen or heard from homeboy and we're embarking upon kindergarten graduation for my daughter. She's set to get a host of awards and she's being honored for wining first place in the Technology Science Fair hosted by the school district in which we currently reside. Everyone is excited for her, especially my family.

Since Kindergarten is a huge milestone for all children I planned a party for all the children in the class. We've had a wonderful group of kids this past year and the teachers were the best of the best! My daughter is reading on third grade level and math is consistent with that of a second grader, again...life is good. The only thing that appeared to be "missing" was homeboy. Since my daughter began to mingle, she started to ask questions about life and just little things in general and I was okay with it until she came home from a sleep over and asked...

"Mommy why doesn't daddy like me?"

I snapped, "What did you just say to me?"

Ivy put her head down and said, "Mommy why doesn't daddy like me?"

I picked her up and rested my forehead on hers, "Daddy loves you, why would you think otherwise?"

4 Miles to Freedom

"Because I don't see him anymore and Jocelyn's dad was there for our picnic and he was nice. We had a water fight."

"Okay, that's because Jocelyn's dad lives with her."

"Well why doesn't daddy live with us?"

"Because he lives somewhere else, Ivy."

"Well where does he live?"

"I don't know. But I tell you what? How about YOU call daddy and ask him if he can pick you up for a movie or something, would you like that?"

"Yes"

"Ok, hand me my cell phone…" and I dialed the only person I knew would give me his new number.

The Final installment of the Kalico Jones Trilogy

4 Miles to Freedom

UNCLE G TO THE RESCUE

Ring…ring…

Ring…ring…

Ring…ring…

Damn, its going to voicemail, I guess I'll have to leave a message, "Hey G, its Mia, if you could please tell homeboy I need his telephone number. His daughter would like to speak with him, thank you." And I left my cell phone number, my work number and even Ivy's cell phone number.

That was 4:30pm on a Saturday. Wednesday G called me back.

Thank GOD it wasn't an emergency.

But thank GOD he didn't do me like homeboy's so-called cousin.

Ring…ring…

I looked at the called I.D. I didn't recognize the number but I did recognize the name, it was G calling me back…good, "Hey there Mr. G, how are things?"

"Good Kal, can't complain, how is my niece?" Since he and homeboy were such good friends, my daughter called him "Uncle" G…which was fine by me.

"She's good G, and how are your children, I know…getting big now, right?"

4 Miles to Freedom

"Yeah, time flies. Little G is walking and talking and Sabrina is sassy, but its all good, you know she's going to seventh grade."

"Really, damn time sure does fly."

"So what's up. I got the message, I spoke to Wisdom, he said I could give you the cell phone number, so here it is...you know he loves his daughter."

Bingo!

There was the "in" I needed to have a conversation about how homeboy has been a deadbeat for three years..."I know you ain't hardly trying to tell me this nigga misses his daughter, you better NOT even go there."

"Listen I ain't getting in the middle of yawls shit, 'cause I think you still love the nigga. I'm just saying, he does love his daughter and you need to cut the bullshit and let him be a father, stop trying to control him through his daughter."

"Oh he got to you too..."

"Nah Kal, he didn't get to me, I just see the look in his eyes when he sees the rest of the crew with our kids, he looks sad."

"Yeah, well he should look sad, he should look pathetic, not seeing his child in 14 months. What part of the game is that? Please make me understand this shit?"

"Listen, let her call her father and call me back. I want to talk to you about what I heard from Richard and his girl."

"Fuck them bum ass motherfuckers. They better not ever ask me shit about my daughter. They can both go to hell...and Adrianne had the nerve to call me a bitch...like she can fight. I couldn't believe my ears."

"Kal let Ivy call her dad and call me back. I'm about to get off work. Give me a half hour to get settled at home and we'll talk."

The Final installment of the Kalico Jones Trilogy

4 Miles to Freedom

I hung up the phone. I looked down at the piece of paper I had written homeboys number on and threw it in the garbage.

9:30pm that same night.

Ring...ring...

Ring...ring...

Ring...

I rolled over. I didn't even look at the called I.D, half asleep I answered the phone, "Hello."

"Kal this is G I have Wisdom on the phone. I think we should get this out in the open. Y'all stop acting like kids. The relationship is over. He wants to see his daughter. Lets talk."

"I'm sleep"

"See that's what the fuck I'm talking about. Shit is always on her fucking time like she's in charge." It was homeboy on the other line yelling and cursing just because I said I was asleep.

Ping!

Now I'm awake. I sat up in bed and began to yell, "Nigga you better not ever talk to me like that. Fuck you. I'm in the bed mother fucker, that's what people do when they are tired, they lay the fuck down... how dare you call my fucking house and interrupt my fucking sleep to be rude. Who in the hell do you think you are?"

"I want to see my daughter! You going around telling niggas I'm a deadbeat. That I don't take care of my daughter, when you're the one who won't let me see her...YOU Kj...YOU...this shit is all YOUR fault...bitch!"

"Did you just call me a bitch? Listen and G you listen too...I don't give a shit if you don't like me. I don't give a shit if I lined up all your friends and suck their dicks in front of you...I AM the mother

4 Miles to Freedom

of your child and if you don't respect me for any other reason other than the fact that I have been doing it BY MY FUCKING SELF for years now...you WILL fucking respect me. You save that bitch shit for your girl, in the meantime, you can try calling again when you grow up...FAG!"And I slammed the phone down. But I didn't hang it up. I actually threw it upside the fucking wall. Chipping my custom interior matte finish paint job...DAMN!

Just then I heard a thump. I ran to Ivy's room. She had fallen out of bed. I picked her up off the floor, I wiped her face, she was crying... "Mommy who were you yelling at?"

Off guard I responded, "Oh baby you must have had a nightmare, mommy wasn't yelling. I was asleep. I heard you fall and I ran in here to make sure you were okay."

"Oh"

I told my first lie to my daughter. Ugh. I felt horrible.

The next day G reached out to me. Or did I reach out to him. Whatever it was, we spoke and he apologized for the conversation and agreed homeboy should not disrespect me because at the end of the day, I AM a good mother and he should be thankful for that. But at the same time, I should not allow myself to be baited into acting out of character.

It was one month prior to my daughter's kindergarten graduation and two months prior to her 6th birthday. I had to finalize the plans for seven parties. One for graduation and six for her birthday...we've gotten into this one for each year routine, which was mostly themed. For example: Tea party, breakfast party, dinner party, party at camp, sleep over, etc. I enjoyed watching the kids have a good time. Stress free...ahh, the beauty of being a carefree kid.

(singing) "Back in the days when I was young...I'm not a kid anymore but some days I sit and wish I was a kid again."(exhaling) So I had a lot of things to accomplish in a short amount of time and so I could not allow homeboy to get me off focus. I agreed with G that I would "behave" during our next try at a dialogue.

The Final installment of the Kalico Jones Trilogy

4 Miles to Freedom

8:30pm

Ring...ring...

I looked at the called i.d. it was G. I knew homeboy would be on the other end and so I told myself I would be the person I know I am and not allow him to have so much control over me to the point where I begin the belittle myself by acting a fool.

Too bad it didn't work.

"Hey Kal, its G. Now we're not going to talk about what happened the other night. We just want to consider that water under the bridge and move on...agreed?"

Both me and homeboy were silent. G repeated himself, "Hello Fam...I said, agreed?"

"Agreed" I responded in a damn near whisper.

Homeboy chimed in, "Agreed."

"Good now Kal we all know you are a good mother, no one can dispute and no one can take that away from you and Wisdom you WERE a good father but for whatever reason you have not been active in your daughter's life here lately. We are trying to resolve that with this call. Kal, when can Wisdom come pick up his daughter?"

"Come pick her up? She hasn't seen him in over one year. He can come visit her. Maybe take her out to lunch or for a movie, but there will be no over night visits."

"Ok that's understandable...Wisdom when would you like to visit your daughter?"

"What do you mean no overnight visits...like I'm going to hurt her or something. I'm the one who used to take her to the doctor. I'm the one who took care of you...AND your family when they needed a place to stay...YOU didn't have to work and so you DIDN'T work. You drove in luxury...you LIVED in luxury...and now you're ungrateful!

4 Miles to Freedom

Niggas told me not to fuck with you and you know what? I should have NEVER fucked with you, let alone have kids with you."

Oh hells to da naw…he fucking went there again. The only thing I said was that there would be no sleep overs. I never said he couldn't spend time with his daughter, Did you hear me say that? Exactly… check out what happens next.

Flick!

He just flicked the bitch switch, "You damn right you took care of me…you knew what I was about when you met me and you toed the line like every other mother fucker…and you're right I didn't work. The cars, the homes, yeah…yeah…yeah…you said all that to say what? When you ain't doing a damn thing now. Nothing to help your daughter. What about what I have done for your black ass?"

"What did you do for me Kj…what?"

"Nigga please, don't act like you don't know…If it weren't for bitches sweating ME… you would get NO pussy. I put you and half of that small ass town on…don't hate because I upgraded my situation. While you running around with every bum ass bitch you can find. And for the record. Those same niggas who told you not to fuck with me, probably tried to kick it to me at one time or another. Go fuck yourself homeboy. G I told you this would not work!"

G yelling, trying to interject… "Hold it…hold it…y'all have to stop this. This shit is dumb. Y'all are both wack. I can't do this. Y'all either need to go to counseling collectively AND individually or y'all need to just fuck and get it over with. I think y'all need to consider these options."

We both were quiet.

G continued, "Now I got my own problems and so I'm not going to sit on the phone and listen to this shit. Wisdom this situation makes me and the crew sad, 'cause you ain't doing the right thing. So let's start over. Kal when can he come get his daughter?"

4 Miles to Freedom

"Whenever he wants."

"Well Wisdom, when do you want to get her?"

"I can come on Friday, but she ain't gonna be there, something will happen where Kj will not be around."

I opened my mouth to respond, "Excuse me...Uh, I'm..."

G jumped right in, "Listen okay now I'm going to make the schedule, Kal, when I get off work Friday, I am going to bring Wisdom out there to see his daughter. Now we're having a bbq on Saturday and so I'm asking you if she can stay overnight."

"I don't have a problem with that. Good I can go out. Friday it is then...oh what time will you guys be here?"

"Around 9pm because I don't get off until 7 and you have to give us time to get over the bridge and through the traffic."

"Well she goes to sleep at 8pm, maybe you should wait until Saturday morning to pick her up."

I heard someone suck their teeth, "Here's goes the bullshit...I told you." Homeboy trying to get G to see his point of view.

"Kal it's Friday, it should be okay if she is picked up past her bedtime. Its not like she has to go to school the next day." G reminded me.

"You're right. You're right. I will see you Friday at 9pm."

I hung up the phone.

I waited a few minutes and called G back and said, "Make sure homeboy knows he is going to have to give me the address and telephone number the place where my child will be staying or she ain't going."

"Well why didn't you keep it real and say that shit while we were all on the phone?"

4 Miles to Freedom

"It didn't cross my mind."

"Ok. Well I'll make sure you get the address, but I gave you the number the other day."

"Yes and I threw it in the garbage."

Laughing G said, "Kal get some sleep, we'll be there on Friday."

And here comes Friday and I waited and I waited and I waited. Ivy was excited and she stayed up…past her bedtime because she didn't want to miss anything. It was like she was waiting to get a glimpse of Santa Claus.

11:42pm

Buzzzzzzz…Buzzzzzzz

Is that my damn bell ringing? I had fallen asleep on the sofa with Ivy laying on top of me. She was sound asleep when her father walked in the G. I gave G a hug and kiss, "Hey Fam, what's up…look a little chunky there, that money must be right, 'cause you're weight is up." And I patted his stomach.

Homeboy walked in behind him. We made eye contact and my heart began to race. Damn baby daddy looks gooood. Damn! Arms were nice and tanned. Shoulders were just as I remembered…My ass was in a trance. I walked over and touched his arms… "Hmmmm, nice… nice…you look good." Did I just say that? Shit there I go again, playing myself.

"You look good too Kj." Homeboy responded.

And here goes G, "That ass is FAT! When did you get those hips?"

"Ha ha very funny G. I got these hips back in 2000 when I pushed out that baby over there. Shhh, she's sleeping. Listen, I know we got off on the wrong foot, but I'm happy she will be spending time with you. Where are you guys going?"

4 Miles to Freedom

"I live in Brooklyn now and my girl has a child the same age as Ivy. We are going to take them out to the skating rink tomorrow."

What happened to the bbq? (I was saying to myself). I should just pull the plug on this shit right now. This nigga ain't seen or spoke to his daughter in 14 months and instead of him spending time with her... he is going to do it with not only a different woman, but a kid too! So he's been taking care of someone else's kid. WOW. Its worst than I thought.

Whatever. It was too late for me to go back on my word. And besides that, Ivy was up and ready to go hang with her Daddy. I took her in the room with me for a minute to talk, "Ivy, here is your cell phone... you are NOT to turn it off. I will chirp you tomorrow morning. When you get to daddy's house, and its time to change into your pjs I want you to go into the bathroom to change and press this button, do you understand me?"

"Yes mommy."

And I handed Ivy the Boost Mobile phone on the GPS tracking screen, ready to be activated. I WAS getting the address whether he left it or not. Yes, I GPS'd my kid. SUE me!

We walked back into the living room. G and homeboy were in Ivy's room looking at the new furniture I had purchased complete with a flat screen television and some sort of gaming system she just had to have. I gave Ivy another hug and kiss. Reminded her to say her prayers and that Jesus loved her and they were off. I closed the door behind them and sat on my sofa and cried. I could not believe I allowed my daughter to go off with someone she hasn't seen in over one year, to a place she has never been. To be around people she didn't know.

Am I nuts or what? Exactly. Nuts!

4 Miles to Freedom

I OPENED A BOTTLE OF CHAMPAGNE POURED MYSELF A GLASS AND DRANK IT, THEN POURED MYSELF ANOTHER GLASS AND DRANK THAT...

I called one of my neighbors and asked for a cigarette. She came downstairs and said, "Kalico Jones what is going on with you...did you drink all this liquor?"

I looked over at her holding up two very empty bottles of Korbel extra dry and I fell on the floor, I was sobbing hysterically... "I should have never let her go...I should have never let her go...I'm so stupid." I began to punch myself in the legs repeatedly.

"Kalico you have to get a grip. Things will be okay. She is with her father, nothing is going to happen. I need to call your mother, what is her number?"

"No! Don't you dare call my mother, she's going to kill me when she finds out I let Ivy go with homeboy, please do not call my mother Shonda, do not."

Just then I heard my cell phone beep. Ivy had activated the GPS function. Good, she must be at her father's house. I let the tracking program run. Jackpot! Location seized. I'm good, but they were not in Brooklyn, they were in Long Island.

Lying ass!

Hold on. Long Island? Wait a second. Let me get the particulars on this location. I called my friend Manny, the police officer I briefly dated back in When Gucci Came First and asked him to help me out.

The Final installment of the Kalico Jones Trilogy

4 Miles to Freedom

Five minutes later he called me back with an absolute street address. Hmmm, now why does this address seem familiar to me. Who in the hell did I know in Long Island? Oh Shit!! No the fuck he didn't!!! No Lawd please tell me he didn't!!!

My daughter was with Mrs. Mattress from Hempstead, Long Island. You remember the one from When Gucci Came First – my so called friend. And my second book And to you homeboy I say thanks – the one who I was going to make my daughter's God Mother…that was her mother's address. Oh someone is going to die tonight! I called G, it went straight to voicemail. I left a message.

"G I am going to kick homeboy's ass. My daughter is NOT in Brooklyn she is in Long Island and I know exactly where. She must be home tomorrow no later than 6pm. She will not be going with him again."

G called me back a few hours later, "Kal you have to calm down, now I thought they were in Brooklyn. I don't know what you are talking about. Why don't you just call him?"

"I can't right now because I am furious. After tomorrow I won't have to deal with this shit and so it's all good. He better cherish this time with her now… 'Because it's a done deal after he drops her off."

Shonda was yelling for me to hang up. My mother was on the other phone and Shonda had informed her of what was going on. Shit. I got on the phone, "Hey Ma, what's up?"

"Kalico Renee Jones, if anything happens to my grand baby…I am going to hurt you, do you understand me?"

"Nothing is going to happen Ma, relax."

"Kalico Renee Jones, if anything happens to my grand baby there will be a police car and an ambulance outside of your house when I get there and I will be getting in the police car!"

"Ma you don't have the threaten me. Ivy will be home by 6pm tomorrow and this won't happen again, I promise."

4 Miles to Freedom

"That's what you say EVERY year and EVERY fucking year, you make this same dumb ass decision to let Ivy go with her dad and every year he cries about how he is going to do right and he hasn't yet...I wonder just what it will take for you to get it."

"Ma...please just relax for one night, that's all I ask."

I didn't hear a response. "Ma...Ma?" Oh shit. She hung up on me. My ass is in trouble. I can't tell you what time I finally went to sleep. The only thing I can tell you is that I woke up at 5:30am to a chirp... it was my daughter.

BLEEP... "MOMMY ARE YOU UP?"

Bleep... "Mommy are you up?"

I grabbed the phone, "Yes baby mommy is up, what's up?"

"Mommy I am hungry and everyone is asleep, I'm thirsty too."

"Okay honey where is daddy?"

"He's in his room."

"And where is the little girl who lives there?"

"She's sleeping. Mommy I'm hungry."

Shit. I'm pissed. I was in a situation. Now if I call the father's cell phone, he is going to know Ivy called me and I didn't want him or anyone else to act funny toward her because of my call. I had 12 and a half hours until my daughter would be arriving and I didn't want it to be a miserable 12 and a half hours for her. "Ivy, do you know where the kitchen is?"

"Yes"

"Well go and get yourself something to drink."

"Okay mommy"

"And take the phone with you...I want you to keep your finger on the button so I can hear you walk to the kitchen, okay?"

"Okay"

4 Miles to Freedom

And Ivy did just what I told her. She kept her finger on the button as she walked to the kitchen and about 15 seconds into her walk to find the kitchen, I heard someone yell, "Get your ass back in the bed, its too early for you to be up!"

Who in the fuck was that?

Ivy said, "But I'm hungry and thirsty."

"I don't care, no one is up, get back to bed, now!"

I didn't hear anything else. I chirped my daughter. Bleep… "Ivy can you hear me?" Bleep… "Ivy can you hear me?"

And a now crying Ivy responded, "Yes mommy"

I said, "Who told you to go back to bed?"

"Daddy's wife."

Ok. I'm going to call him, keep the phone by you. Give me a minute to call you back.

Ring…ring…

Ring…ring…

Shit its going to voicemail.

I called again.

Ring…ring…

Ring…ring…

Shit its going to voicemail again.

I called again.

Ring…ring…

The Final installment of the Kalico Jones Trilogy

4 Miles to Freedom

Ring…ring…

And a sleep homeboy answered, "Yeah"

I said in a loud tone, "This is Kj, your daughter is crying, she is hungry and thirsty. This is the time she gets up in the morning. Get your ass up and fix her something to eat. Give her crackers if you have them to hold her over until you get up and make sure you give her something to drink. And tell your girlfriend I'm going to kick her ass when I catch her for cursing at my daughter. I don't do it and she isn't going to do it."

"What the fuck are you talking about?"

"I heard her tell Ivy to take her ass back to bed."

"Well I'm sure she didn't mean it like that. Like I'm sure she wasn't being mean."

"Nigga are you dumb or are you stupid. NO one should speak to a child like that. There was no need to curse. When I catch her, her ass belongs to me. Please let her know," and I hung up.

I called Ivy back.

Bleep… "Ivy are you there?"

"Yes mommy"

"Daddy should be coming to fix you breakfast if not, then you go knock on his door, okay?"

"Okay"

And that was the last time I heard from my daughter. Until 10:30 that night when he dropped her off. Four and a half hours late. He turned her cell phone off. His excuse for being late, "She was having dinner" and he "lost track of time."

My daughter had two bloodshot eyes and a nasty rash when she got

4 Miles to Freedom

home. That Monday her school called me stating she appeared "withdrawn." I kept her home and out of school AND the public, for the remainder of the week. I was afraid they would call Child Protective Services.

My daughter's teacher called my house to find out where Ivy was and what was going on. I told her why I hadn't been sending her to school. She told me that I was worrying about nothing and that she would never call child protective services on me because she knows the behavior Ivy displayed was not a reaction to something I had done.

Thank GOD!

The Final installment of the Kalico Jones Trilogy

4 Miles to Freedom

WHERE DID ALL THESE PEOPLE COME FROM?

In the meantime graduation and her birthday were quickly approaching. My job was asking for a lot of over time and life seemed to resume. We had not heard from homeboy and didn't bother calling. But we did hear from everyone else. If it wasn't through MySpace, it was from people being able to now "Google" Kalico Jones and get all my information. At one point even my telephone number. My world began to appear small, as people from my past began to surface.

First Mike Boogie, you remember him from When Gucci Came First, right? Well I ran into him during Harlem week. I was out signing books and handing out promo items to the crowd when I recognized him.

"Mike...Mike..."

He turned around with this look like "Who is this person calling me?"

I didn't give him a chance to ask that question, I immediately yelled, "Its Kj...from Mt. Vernon."

"Oh shoot, little KJ from Mt. Vernon...I heard you wrote a book and I'm in it."

"Yeah, yeah...as a matter of fact, here's a complimentary copy for you, sir."

He reached out his hand to take the book. There was a women standing behind him in the distance, who I later found out was his wife. I pulled back my hand and said, "You can have this book on one condi-

The Final installment of the Kalico Jones Trilogy

4 Miles to Freedom

tion… you must let me take a photo of you holding it up…you know, for my promo page and all."

He agreed and obliged my request. We exchanged numbers and had several long conversations about life and the pursuit of happiness after that and even made plans to meet for dinner and drinks. But once I found out he had befriended Kelly in the recent months, I decided not to go there. I just didn't want to have anything to do with anyone who had anything to do with her. No offense, but I know my limitations. But it was nice to see him though and I hear he's doing very well for himself. I wish him and his family the best!

In the meantime and in between time Mt. Vernon had began to take center state in my life in that again, between MySpace and Google people who read my books began to track me down.

I checked my yahoo account, kalicojones@yahoo.com

857 emails in one day! Ugh. Let me skim down the list…bookstores, bookstores, bookstores…ski trips…Oh here's one from Talent. He's hosting yet another comedy showcase…he's got to be the hardest working man in show business…here's one from Mike L…what in the hell is cousin L up to? Oh shit, that's right. I did reach out to Big T a few weeks back, this must be in reference to that, I'll just give him a call later. Hmm…PayPal payment notification notice. Oh someone purchased a book from my MySpace page. Let's see who this is…I opened my email, "RHONDA!!!" What in the fuck did SHE want with a copy of my book? I guess someone asked her about that drink incident in When Gucci Came First – whatever.

I sent a response email, "Thank you for your recent purchase. A copy of the first installment of the Kalico Jones Trilogy, When Gucci Came First is being shipped via federal express next day air to you compliments of Miss Kali Jones, enjoy your read."

And she shot back and email saying, "Mia I want to speak with you."

"Mia" no she didn't call me by my REAL name.

WOW. I'm baffled.

The Final installment of the Kalico Jones Trilogy

4 Miles to Freedom

She even sent her home telephone number.

After one week of looking at that same email, I called Rhonda to find out what in the world she wanted with me and it happened...

She gossiped about everyone and everything. What she heard about me. What she heard about my family. How people were hating on me because of my books. And how Cee Cee said she would fight me no matter when or where she sees me because I mentioned fucking her baby daddy in my book.

Whatever...and get over it...BITCH and besides that, do you think I only know ONE fucking Cee Cee? Ugh the nerve! And the gossip, well I'm not going to sit here and say I didn't listen, because I DID. I listened to all of it, even inquiring as to the whereabouts of homeboy and what she may have heard and...

She told me all of his business too.

I knew everything.

Rhonda was a blabber mouth and I loved every bit of it. A couple of times a week, Rhonda and I would be on the phone gabbing about shit that didn't have a damn thing to do with us. I had moved back to Mt. Vernon mentally.

Everyone had my number and I had their number too. My life began to be a three ring circus because I was getting caught up in he said she said at my fucking old age. Bitches were calling me on the phone talking shit, it was a mess. Here I am this phenom...I'm KALICO JONES and I was allowing my past to be my present.

It was two more weeks until my daughters Kindergarten graduation and I hadn't planned shit. I was so wrapped up in everyone's life and what was going on back there in Mt. Misery...oops, I mean Mt. Vernon. What homeboy was up to. Who he was fucking and who was wearing what at the party. To put it in plain English, I cared about dumb shit.

I knew it was bad when homeboy's mother called me. Beep. (I was on

4 Miles to Freedom

the other line trying to straighten out some shit I didn't say for the fifth time that week), "Listen I have to call you back. I have another call and I have to go."

I clicked over to a yelling homeboy's mother, "Kj you keep my name out of your fucking mouth…do you hear me?"

"What…who IS this?"

"This is homeboy's mother…and I heard what you've been saying about me and my son. I read those fucking books, you better stop it and I'm not playing. You know he has sisters."

"Are you threatening me? 'Cause that means nothing. Why are you mad, 'because I called him a deadbeat, he IS. I mean he should hold his head up and be proud. These are his actions. Not mine. I just stated the facts."

"Well God don't like ugly and it will come back to you."

"Well instead of you yelling at me, why are you NOT speaking with your son? Ask him why he's a deadbeat and try to encourage him to do better…as a matter of fact, none of you have even called my daughter to see how she was doing. She's been sick. I call you people and you don't respond. Her graduation is coming. I know you got the party invites, 'because I sent seven to your son and I have yet to hear from you guys. Christmas, Thanksgiving, Family reunions, don't y'all realize someone is missing?"

"Hold on…what are you talking about young woman?"

"I'm talking about you guys not showing my daughter any type of love. Nothing."

"I've sent her plenty of gifts, even jewelry. I've even sent money a few times. You mean to tell me you haven't gotten anything from my son?"

"No"

The Final installment of the Kalico Jones Trilogy

4 Miles to Freedom

"So you've just been thinking we don't care?"

"Basically."

"Well that's not true. I have to get off the phone with you. I need to call my son, but I will be calling you back." A few hours later she called my house again. This time her tone was different. We spoke for a few hours. She even spoke with my daughter. I had a positive outlook as to the direction this entire fiasco could go…Every day she would call to find out if I needed anything for the party. Of course I said no. Each night Ivy would go to be after being serenaded over the phone by her other grandmother, it was nice. Homeboy started calling. He was respectful, I really felt it was a nice new start.

And then…

Homeboys mother called my house with, "Kj I need a favor…I need you to remove my son from child support." (exhaling) ok here's the bullshit. I knew it…I knew it.

"I don't know if that would be a smart thing for me to do."

"Well you're not getting it anyway and really, back in the day, I never considered taking his father to court for child support. I handled my own business. If you need something I will help you. Right now my son needs to get his life together and he cant do that with child support on his back, he's going to lose his license again, which means his job will follow."

And without thinking I agreed to take him off child support. I called the case worker to find out what was needed from me to make it happen. I was told a letter. I wrote the letter and put it in an envelope. The next day when his mother called I told her it was ready and asked where I should mail it. She told me that homeboy had planned to attend his daughter's graduation and that I could give it to him then.

Oh shoot. He's actually going to be there for his daughter? Let me not complain. This was a good thing, right?

4 Miles to Freedom

GRADUATION FELL ON A WEDNESDAY

And was now four days away. My Aunt offered to make a cake, but I had to go to Harlem to pick it up the night before the event. I spent Sunday and Monday having CDs burned for my daughter to hand out as graduation gifts to her entire class. You should have seen the CD covers I designed. Parents were talking about them for weeks after. So between burning cds, negotiating contracts with the illustrator for my daughter's book, The Dinosaur and Silva, my full time job AND last minute dress shopping with my mother, (exhaling) it was a busy couple of days.

I threw on a Dior baseball cap, jumped in my car and headed to Harlem. I had to pick up the cake from my grandmother's house. I was dirty...had not showered (YUCK), it was hot out and I had to be back in jersey in ONE hour and so I couldn't stay. I entered Lakeview and pressed for the elevator.

My cell phone rang.

"Hello this is Kali"

"Hey this is homeboy, did you write the letter?"

"Hello to you too, and yes, the letter is here, why are you no longer coming to the graduation? You want me to mail it?"

"Nah, nah...I'm coming...I just wanted to remind you because my mother said you were busy running around getting things together for the party."

"Yeah I'm in Harlem right now at my grandmother's house picking

The Final installment of the Kalico Jones Trilogy   39

4 Miles to Freedom

up the cake my aunt made."

"I would have done that. Don't you have a dress fitting today?"

"Yes in one hour and so I have to make it back. Well I'm in the elevator so the phone is going to cut off...I will call you when I get back across the bridge."

"Ok. Be safe."

Be safe? I would have done that for you...he MUST want something. He was being too nice. Kj stop it. You guys are getting along. Just leave it alone.

I kissed my grandmother, grabbed the cake and got back on the elevator. As I looked up to press the button for the lobby. Someone said, "What's up Renee, you ain't speaking?"

It was Mr. Diamond Bracelet from When Gucci Came First...

Oh shit. I thought to myself, I hope he didn't read the book. If so, this elevator ride may be a not so good experience for me. I mean I did say the dude smelled and looked homeless to have all that money. Damn...

I leaned over and gave him a kiss on the cheek, "What's up Dude, I heard you had a baby..."

"Yeah since you had all those abortions on me...I had to make sure one got to this world."

"Oh don't give me that shit. You knew I wasn't having a kid at that time, but what's up...you look good. That means the money is on target, what's up...Can I have 500 dollars?"

Laughing, "Renee you are never going to change. You know you can get anything from me" as he began to sift through the stack of money in his pocket. He handed me 300 dollars, "And how's your daughter and Momma Lynn?"

4 Miles to Freedom

"They are both good. My daughter graduates from kindergarten tomorrow and my aunt made the cake for the party. What's your number? You should stop by one day...you know I moved, right?"

"Yeah, I ran into Charlie and he told me. Here take my cell number and call me sometime before the weekend. I will be O.T. (out of town) for a few weeks beginning Saturday."

"You still throwing bricks at the precinct? Aren't you too old for that now? And with being a father...Nigga you need do find a job and do forty hours like the rest of the niggas who left the game."

"You know that ain't for me...by the way that Lasagna still tight?"(He was asking about my pussy) WOW. That was his name for it.

"What do you think mother fucker?"

"Doing back shots yet?"

"You know I don't get down like that. That right there is for bitches with pussy problems. I'm barely giving head."

He laughed and we exited the elevator.

I jumped back in my car and headed for Jersey.

My little ones dress was ready and so was mine. I paid for his services – Tyrone of Sew Fast in Bloomfield, NJ and we left. Graduation day was beautiful. The weather was great and we looked fantastic (Thanks again Tyrone!!!). All my close friends were there and family. Ivy looked like a princess. The ceremony began.

No homeboy.

They started calling the children up by class to perform.

No homeboy.

The school principal gave out the awards.

4 Miles to Freedom

Ivy had FIVE.

No homeboy.

Now it was time to give out the diplomas. The ceremony was ending.

Still... NO homeboy.

I walked around the auditorium. I couldn't sit still. It was time for my baby's name to be called. I looked around and made eye contact with my mother, who gave me the "I told you so" look and shook her head in disgust.

NO homeboy.

My girlfriends rallied around me, as I tried not to cry. I can't believe this mother fucker didn't show. This is awful. My daughter was looking forward to it. It was her turn to walk across the stage to receive her diploma. We all stood up. And of course, I yelled, "That's my baby!!!"

As the entire class rose to take a bow before leaving the stage, I looked to the back of the auditorium and there his ass was. I walked over to him. And brought him up front so his daughter could see him. She almost jumped out of the chair.

I handed him the bag of CDs and said, "Do you mind handing these out with Ivy to her classmates while I take a backseat so she can show her father off?"

"Nah, it's all good."

And I let them do their thing. The teachers, parents and children were happy to meet him. And each of them said the same thing, "You have a beautiful daughter, inside and out, you should be very proud."

Yeah right.

4 Miles to Freedom

After the ceremony we had lunch and he dropped us back home. We were walking to our building when he yelled, "Kj, I need the letter."

"Oh shoot, my bad...wait a sec let me get it."

I ran in the house and retrieved it from my purse. I came back out, handed it to him and said, "I hope you live up to your end of the agreement."

And I walked away.

He didn't call that night.

Neither did his mother.

I guess that's all they really wanted.

4 Miles to Freedom

CHEERS TO THE REAL FATHERS... MOTHERS!

That Sunday was Fathers day and I was in the house with my girl Tawana, laughing and joking about how now that I've relinquished homeboy from his financial obligations, my daughter wouldn't get shit. No visits, no calls and now...No money. I decided that it would be his lost if he did us like that...NOT ours. I had a great job and was now in a financial position to make things happen with or without his ass.

I called G.

Ring...ring...

"Hey Jones what's cracking?"

"Nothing G, you heard from homeboy?"

"Nah, the last I heard he was moving, that was it."

"Moving, so he's not with the girl anymore?"

"Nope. And don't ask me what he's up to, 'cause I have no idea."

"Don't worry, I'm not about to go there."

"Oh yeah, he told me my niece was the cutest kid at the graduation. He said you've done a good job with her."

"Really? HE gave ME a compliment."

"Yeah, so what's up?"

4 Miles to Freedom

"Nothing I just called to say Happy Fathers day and keep up the good work, that's all."

"Did you call my man?"

"Nope and we're not going to. He didn't win any father of the year awards this go around and so the answer to your question is no, nor do I have any intentions of allowing my daughter to call him."

"Ok then...well my mother is having a fathers day dinner and so I'm getting ready to go over there...hit me back later."

"Okay, well tell everyone I said hi. Kiss the kiddies for me."

And I hung up. Tawana poured another glass of champagne and gave a toast, "To the REAL fathers...MOTHERS!" We tapped glasses and the phone rang. I looked at the caller I.D., it was homeboy.

Tawana answered the phone, "Hello Kj's house, who's speaking?"

"Can I speak to Ivy?"

"Who is this calling for a child, please?"

"Its her father."

Tawana muffled the phone and whispered, "He asked to speak with Ivy, what do you want me to say?"

"Just give her the phone T"

And she called Ivy to the phone.

About one minute into conversation, Ivy says, "Mommy why didn't you tell me it was Fathers day...you didn't send Daddy the presents I got him!"

"No I didn't because he was supposed to be here on Friday to pick you up for the weekend and he didn't show or call."

4 Miles to Freedom

"Well daddy wants to speak with you." And she passed me the phone.

"Yeah, what's up?"

"What happened to us?"

"What did you just ask me?"

"What happened to us...we had it all...everything was good and now we have nothing."

"Speak for yourself, I'm good!"

"I did everything for you. Everything" (His voice was getting louder with each word. I knew this conversation was going to turn UGLY),

"You happened to US. Blame yourself for this shit Wisdom."

"I blame you. You ruined my life."

"Nigga I was your life. YOUR potential left with me and your daughter. Don't try to make me feel guilty 'cause shit is a mess for you right now...that is not my fault. I released you from child support, which was probably one of the dumbest things I've ever done, 'cause I know your ass ain't gonna do the things you said and mighty funny I haven't heard from your mother since I gave you that letter."

"Don't talk about my mother and you're right. Since you tell everyone I'm a deadbeat, I'm going to BE a deadbeat! You ain't getting shit from me now. Fuck you."

"No...fuck YOU!"

"That's why I'm taking you to court to see my daughter."

"And that's exactly what you will need to do if you want to see her... with your bum ass...goodbye!"

And I changed my home and cell phone numbers the following day.

4 Miles to Freedom

Which is why the case worker assigned to our child support case called my job on Tuesday…

(singing) "GOD DON'T LIKE UGLY... HE'S GONNA MAKE YOU PAY...FOR WHAT YOU'VE DONE TO ME..."

"Mrs. Jones, I am calling because although the respondent (homeboy) dropped off the letter you wrote relinquishing him from child support, We cannot use it."

"Really, why...I included everything you told me to put, what happened?"

"It must be notarized. Now we can still process your request, but you have to send the notarized letter in asap."

Damn, life really is a circle (what goes around comes around). "Sorry, but I wont be doing that now. I've changed my mind. Sorry for taking up your time."

"Okay Mrs. Jones, I will call the respondent (homeboy) and let him know he is still in the system, have a blessed day."

"You too and thank you."

Hooray...lets see how his ass feels now. I immediately called my cousin L.A. to tell her what happened, "Good now please Kj, move on with your life. Leave his ass alone. Please promise me you will leave him alone."

"I promise."

Yeah right.

It was back to life as I knew it.

4 Miles to Freedom

Knock...knock...knock...

What the fuck! Who gained access into my building without my knowledge. I looked through the peep hole to see who was at the door. It was the mailman with a package. I opened the door. The package was addressed to my daughter. There was no return address.

Hmmm, that's peculiar. I opened it in the presence of the mail carrier. It was a children's Bible book and a card attached, "Congratulations to our middle school graduate!"

What?

Who in the fuck sent this? I opened to the card. To Ivy, spelled IN-CORRECT... "As you begin high school remember the golden rule Books before Boys! Love Granny"

Middle school graduate?

Books before boys?

Name spelled wrong?

Ugh...how do you confuse a Kindergarten graduation with someone going off the high school? I went next door to Tawana's house.

Knock...Knock... "Open the door T, is Kali!"

With a scarf on her head... "What bitch you know I sleep to Noon."

I handed her the card, "Girl read this and tell me what you make of it."

"I make of it that it was the only card left in the dollar store...I make of it that the person who sent it did not care to know the correct spelling of your daughter's name. I make of it, that if it were me, I'd correct it and send it back."

"It came from homeboy's side of the family."

The Final installment of the Kalico Jones Trilogy

4 Miles to Freedom

"Word?" and Tawana busted into laughter..., "That family can't stand your ass Jones...they can't stand you."

"Well that's all I wanted to show you. Go back to bed and come over when you get up. I'm cooking lunch in a few and cleaning."

"Ok."

And I went back to my apartment to sweep up the dirt by the living room entry way. I opened the card, bent down and swept the pile of dirt in it and threw it in the trash. Yes...I used it as a dustpan. I gave my daughter the Bible stories, of which she enjoys to this day.

In the meantime I begin my show on www.artistfirst.com it's a LIVE internet broadcast with over 50 thousand listeners worldwide...I like it and my fan base is growing. The Kalico Jones show. Between the books, my job, being a mother, my daughter's book and the show I am swamped. After eight weeks of working without a day off, I decided to get dressed and take my black ass out on the town.

I called my brother Joey who volunteered to take his niece for the weekend, "Hey Joey, what's up?"

"Nothing...what's up with you Kali...you must want something and I ain't giving you money for you to spend on whatever handbag is hot to you right now, so don't think about it."

"Joey...I need you to take your niece for the weekend, I want to go out."

"I thought homeboy was going to be taking her for the weekends as part of that sorry arrangement mommy told me y'all made."

"Let's not talk about that."

"What...let me guess...he ain't showed up yet?"

"Nope, but I know you will...so be here Friday when you get off work. I will have her bag packed."

The Final installment of the Kalico Jones Trilogy

4 Miles to Freedom

"Ok. I will see you on Friday and make sure your ass is home Sunday morning, 'cause we'll be bringing her back early in the morning...so don't be out partying like you don't have responsibilities, you hear me?"

"I heard you...see you Friday!"

Now I have a reason to shop. I got dressed, picked Ivy up from a play date and we headed to B. Goodman. I looked down at my daughter...

"Ahh, I love my life!"

The Final installment of the Kalico Jones Trilogy

YOU...ME AND HE... WHAT WE GONNA DO BABY?

After B. Goodman we sat down to a sushi dinner at a restaurant overlooking Central Park. The scenery was grand, as was the service.

My cell phone rang.

Ring...ring...

Ugh, I hate when people call me while I'm out having dinner with my daughter, its so intrusive...but I guess since they don't know...you cant hold them at fault. It was my girl P, she was calling to tell me her Vegas trip had been cut short and she needed me to meet me at the airport with her car.

"P, I cant drive to your house, pick up your car, drive to the airport, go back to your house to drop you, go home, AND meet my date on time."

"Bitch when did YOU start caring about being on time for a nigga... don't play me, play lotto."

"P, he's not just some date, its Eric."

"Eric...hold on...isn't he MARRIED?"

"Yes, but he and his wife haven't been together in about three years, she's even relocated. I believe they are in the process of getting a divorce."

"That's what every nigga says when he wants a piece of ass on the side. Girl I can't believe you are actually going to take it there, haven't y'all

4 Miles to Freedom

been friends for years?"

"15 years and that's all the more better."

"No…what you MEANT to say was that's all the more reason why you shouldn't do it…don't say shit when its over and y'all are not speaking, his wife wants to kick your ass and y'all fuck up the friendship."

"Oh shut up."

"Shut up NOW…Oh my God P why didn't you talk me out of it LATER."

"Whatever"

"Well since it's just Eric, I don't understand why you can't pick me up from the airport…come on Kali… please."

"Ok P, WE will pick you up, what time does your flight get in?"

"7:30pm"

"See you at 7:30pm then."

I hung up and resumed my mommy and daughter dinner. Or so I thought. I looked up and Ivy had gone to sleep. WOW, was I on the phone that long? I picked her up and headed for the car service waiting in the lobby to transport us back to Jersey. We arrived home safe and sound. Good.

I put my daughter in her bed, kissed her on the cheek and closed her room door behind me and the bell rang. I thought to myself, "Is this disturb the shit out of Kj day?" I opened the door and it was Eric. I gave him a kiss on the cheek.

"What a nice surprise, to what do I owe the honor, sir?"

"Cut it out Kal, I wanted to see you. I've been thinking a lot about our talk the other day and our upcoming date. I just wanted to see you."

The Final installment of the Kalico Jones Trilogy

4 Miles to Freedom

"Well come in. Did you eat? You know I can whip up something for you."

"Nah, I'm not hungry."

I began to remove my blouse.

"Uh...Uh, so what did you do today, how was your mommy and me dinner?"

"It was wonderful, then P called talking about how her black ass needs to be picked up from the airport. I told her we would do it."

"P is nuts...her trip is kind of short this go around, her Vegas man must be getting sick of tricking."

"Ha ha ha...NOT funny and don't talk about my girl. She's making the dough go nuts. She has no children, she SHOULD run around for a minute, what's wrong with that? And besides, it ain't tricking if you got it to spend!"

Eric moved toward me. I was standing in the hallway topless with panty hose. I had removed my skirt during his joke about my friend. He put his arms around my waist, "I'm glad you're finished running. I've waited 15 years to get you Kal and I won't let you go."

I hugged him back and we kissed, his hands were moving into the no trespassing zone, "Boy if you don't get your hands from out of my ass, it's gonna be ON!" We started laughing, I continued, "Well make yourself comfortable, I am going to take a quick shower, give me ten minutes."

And fifteen minutes later when I got out of the shower, I returned to the living room in my towel, to find that Eric was gone.

What the fuck?

I picked up the phone and dialed his cell phone number. I knew he could not have made it home that quick.

4 Miles to Freedom

He picked up on the fourth ring.

"Eric?"

"What's up baby?"

"Why did you leave, I told you to give me ten minutes."

"Nah, I just didn't want to bother you. I know I just popped up. I felt like I was intruding on your space."

"Did I say you were intruding on my space?"

"No"

"And so why did you feel the need to leave...let me make this clearer...I wasn't READY for you to leave."

He was silent.

I guess he was trying to figure out what I meant by that, but he knew. He and I had been playing hide and seek with each other for over 15 years.

"Eric, did you hear me? I said I wasn't ready for you to leave."

"Uuuhhh, do what do you want me to do?"

"I want you to get your ass back over here."

"Uuuuhhh okay, I'll be there in a few minutes."

I ran around the house looking for my absolute favorite perfume, Insurrection and sprinkled it around the back of my ear and earlobes. I sprayed some on a finger and rubbed it around my "personal spots" – took a bottle of Suave limited edition Caramel scented lotion and gave myself a quick rub down. Added a little Vaseline across da booty and found a gorgeous Kimono in red with a pair of Jimmy Choo shoes. Can you say Dee-LISH? I looked and smelled good. I was ready for this encounter. I guess I was just looking forward to being with some-

The Final installment of the Kalico Jones Trilogy

4 Miles to Freedom

one after the long hard road to freedom from my dear ex. Although I have dated and in some cases considered to be in a "relationship" with the person, I could never get too serious because my heart was back in Mt. Vernon.

Was I actually ready to give up "da goods" to Eric after being his friend, buddy and confidant for so many years? Our families were meshed by the friendship we built as well. I guess I was about to find out.

Eric rang the bell and I opened the door. Looked him in the eyes and said, "Wanna play?"

He picked me up and kissed me all the way to my bedroom. We undressed each other and just laid there talking about how we first met. It was a nice time. No sex, just conversation about goals and dreams and how I was REALLY feeling about being a single parent.

Eric UNDERSTOOD me.

Each night that followed, Eric would pick me up from work, take me to pick up my daughter, of whom he had a friendship with prior. I told you Eric has been around my family for over 15 years. His children and my daughter have played together and so Ivy seeing him was nothing NOTICEABLE. We made sure that intimacy was strictly private. Not even hand holding was "allowed" in the presence of my daughter.

Since Eric and I are no longer together, after about ten months of dating, I am not going to go any further than to say. After a few months of allowing him to go back and forth between me and his wife, I decided to open up my end of our relationship…Well I think that's unfair and not totally true. I met someone "Mo" and decided to give Eric an ultimatum, "Leave home girl or date me knowing I am dating others." He chose to continue to date me knowing I would be with someone else.

Translation: "Bitch if you want to be a whore, go right ahead as long as you keep giving me the pussy." I mean that is what he was saying, right?

Yeah, don't act like you don't know.

4 Miles to Freedom

So in the meantime of me dating Eric...I met Mo and he was totally single, never been married, one kid – who was damn near grown, had a great job and was fine fine FINE with all capital letters. Skin was soft like cotton and not far from it in color either, Mo was Puerto Rican. Sexual tension between Mo and I was insatiable, as he knew exactly where to touch me... you could tell he knew his way around a woman. At times being with him was so good, I would lose my train of thought. I remember one time I got up and called my girlfriend P and said, "Bitch I wish I could give him to you for Christmas!" THAT'S how good Mo was to me.

Up until I told him about Eric. Once I told him that there were TWO of them (Eric and Himself) he changed. He began to always find a reason to come to my place. He lived in NYC but that didn't stop him, I would be leaving the office and Mo would be outside my job. A few times he would be outside my job an hour before I was scheduled to get off work and I would have to call Eric and ask him not to come. And my life was like that for months. THREE months of juggling two very determined men. I'm exhausted just off the recollection.

Eric would take me to work. Mo would pick me up and take me home, each day I would say Good morning to Eric and Good Night to Mo and each day my life began to appear increasingly chaotic and since both of them knew when I was with the other, my ass knew it wouldn't be too long before one of them showed up when they had no business and I would be forced to make a choice. But I didn't want to do that. I had two of the best men in my life and I was happy.

I looked at my watch, "Oh shit, Mo is going to come here in twenty minutes to get me, I have to get Eric out now" so I started to tell Eric I was going out and he had to leave.

"Where are you going Kali?"

"I'm going to the mall with P, I have to find a pair of shoes for my big meeting over at RSMG next week."

Eric walked over to me and looked me in the eyes and asked me again, "Where are you going Kali?"

The Final installment of the Kalico Jones Trilogy   57

4 Miles to Freedom

I turned my head, walked away and muttered, "I'm going to the mall with P, why Eric?"

"'Cause you're fucking lying to me right now. You are actually standing in your OWN house, Miss Single woman I can do what I want when I want... and you are lying to me, why?"

"If you know I am lying why ask me again? I am going out. I don't owe you an explanation, that was the deal, Don't ask me shit and I wont ask you if you're still fucking your wife when you go to visit your kids for weeks at a time, right? That was the deal, right?"

Eric left out, but not before he slammed my door. It was so loud, I thought he broke it off the hinges.

Thirty five minutes later Mo calls me saying he is outside and that he wouldn't be coming in since we were running late. We were going to see a movie and have dinner at this new place called the Jerk Pit in Montclair, NJ. I grabbed my cell phone, my purse and put my hand on the door knob to turn it and as I pulled to open the door, I saw Eric coming up the stairs out of the basement of the building. He was going to follow me outside to meet Mo!

Oh hell no I cant have this. I am way too old for this shit and too in control – or so I thought – of my very grown ass situation for me to let Eric stop me from going out or possibly initiate or provoke an altercation with Mo. I grabbed his jacket and yelled, "Nigga I know you ain't hardly gonna follow me out this door, with your married ass. If you follow me out, its over. And I wont tell you not to call 'cause you know how I get down, I will have all my numbers changed in less than an hour...do NOT follow me out this door."

"I love you and I'm sick of you playing me Kali...sick of it."

"Eric I never played you. I told you I was going to date someone. If you really love me. You would just let me go. This man is single and wants the same things I want. If you love me, and you know in your heart you are not divorcing your wife, then please, just let me go."

And I walked out the building to Mo's car and got in it.

4 Miles to Freedom

I didn't hear from Eric for three weeks.

During those three weeks, Mo and I were every where. You could find us around town taking long walks, while holding hands. That's the type of man he was. A hand holder. A man who wanted to show his woman off. He encouraged the dresses and heels. He encouraged the three times per week hair salon visits. He enjoyed the Gucci bag habits and the Tiffany & Co bangles and earrings...he encouraged it, applauded it AND bankrolled it. And me, well I enjoyed it, ALL of it. And its not that Eric didn't win any sponsor of the year awards with me because he did. He gave me whatever I asked for. Whatever. It was just that he came with the sort of baggage that stays...the wife. The kids. You know...the sort of shit stays.

'CAUSE IM HALF CRAZY...THINKING ABOUT YOUR LOVE..
HALF CRAZY

4 Miles to Freedom

'CAUSE I'M HALF CRAZY...THINKING ABOUT YOUR LOVE...HALF CRAZY

CRASH!

I jumped up out of my daughter's bed. Ran out of her room, closed and locked her door behind me. Someone had just broken into my ground floor garden apartment and I didn't want them to harm my daughter. I ran to where I heard the noise, it was the living room. I turned on the light to find a very drunk Eric laying on the floor crying, "Kali I don't care...call the police, I will go to jail to prove my love. I cant stand you being with this nigga. What did I do to you for you to just flip like this?"

I was furious. I yelled, "How did you get in my fucking house Eric... how did you get in my house!"

I picked my cell phone up off the charger and called my mother, it was 3:42am EASTER Sunday morning. WOW

She picked up the phone on the second ring.

Yelling, "Mommy Eric just broke into my fucking house!"

"What Kal?"

"Eric just broke into my house Ma."

"Put his ass on the phone right now!"

As I told you, our families have a great relationship because we've been friends for so many years. Right now he can go to my mother's house and go in the fridge and put his feet up on the sofa.

4 Miles to Freedom

"I cant put him on the phone, 'cause he's drunk and laying on the living room floor crying." I put the phone on speaker.

"Eric, get out of my daughters house right now. She has a child there and you would not like it if someone did that to your kid's mother, get out of her house!"

"But I love her ma and she didn't want to give me any more pussy. She teased me with it and took it away. I love her and I'm not leaving."

I cant believe this nigga just told my mother that shit. Oh LAWD. (shaking my head just thinking about it. I mean really he told my mother I didn't want to give him pussy! I wonder what she was thinking when he said that. Probably "My daughter KJ the damn freak every time she opens the legs we know 'cause some shit happens."

"If you don't leave by the time I get there, I'm going to call the police myself. Now get the fuck out of Kali's house making all that noise with my grand baby there …get your ass out now!"

And Eric got his drunk ass up off my floor and began to call someone from his cell phone.

"Baby…baby, you up?"

Is this nigga retarded or what? He's calling some chick baby after he just broke into my house and cried for me to be with him. Lawd have mercy, this was beginning to mirror some sad ass soap opera. Or so I thought, because with that phone call came…

THE JERRY SPRINGER SHOW!!!!

THIS NIGGA CALLED HIS WIFE!

Not only did he confess to her about me, but he also told her I was pregnant, told her that the reason he was at my house was because I didn't want to give him any more pussy. Did you hear me? Yep, this Nigga told his wife the entire story. He told her that I was cheating on him with "some Puerto Rican mother fucker" and that he was trying to win me back.

The Final installment of the Kalico Jones Trilogy

4 Miles to Freedom

I snatched his cell phone from his hand and hung up. His wife called back immediately. You could hear her screaming through the phone as he attempted to tell this woman that he no longer wanted to be married.

WOW.

"Eric get out of my house!"

I could hear my daughter banging on her bedroom door yelling to be let out.

Oh my goodness...there's way too much shit going on.

After five minutes of listening to my daughter go nuts over being locked in her room, I called my mother again and she told Eric that she was going to call his father if he didn't leave.

He left.

I unlocked my daughter's bedroom door.

Crying, "Mommy are you okay?" Ivy asked.

"Yeah Weenie, I'm good. That was Eric, he's a little upset, but he'll be okay. Lets go back to bed."

He'll be just fine...Yeah right, 'cause his ass was now calling both my home and cell phones simultaneously.

I answered, "What the fuck do you want Eric? You've done enough damage for one day. Go home to your wife and kids."

"Kali I have my wife on the phone. I'm telling her that I love you and I want to be with you. She doesn't believe me. Please tell her I just broke into your house."

I paused, and looked around because for a few short moments I honestly thought someone was going to jump out from one of the closets and yell, "You've been punked!" but no...that didn't happen.

4 Miles to Freedom

Just then and before I could speak, because although I am not a punk bitch, I just didn't know what I could or should say to this women who has known of my existence her entire existence. She's known me and my family as Eric's closest friends. I mean really…what was I supposed to say?

Just as I had gotten a few words together in my mind, a very faint mousey type tone came across the phone lines, "Kj I just want to ask one question, if you knew you wanted him all this time, why watch him be married three times and have four children before you acted on what you were feeling?"

"I have nothing to say. I cant apologize because I am not sorry. He told me you guys were not together and I believed him. I mean you live on the other side of the country for goodness sake. Why would I think he was lying?"

Eric interjected, "Because I wasn't. We haven't gotten along in years. It wasn't just you KJ …there has been other women before you and if you don't want me it will be others after you."

"Eric shut up!" The faint mousey voice was no more, this was now the voice of a woman who just had a rug pulled from under her. This was now the voice of a woman who was examining her options. She continued, "You can have him 'cause he ain't gonna have shit when I get through with him, I'm taking everything. So have fun helping him get it all back."

And right then and there I chose to stand by my friend of 15 years and forgo the situation at hand …I said, "Oh well, then Eric, lets get it back. 'cause I am not going to see him destitute. From the way I see it, here is a man who does not want you. Lets not make this a Kali thing. This is a YOU thing because you don't do your job as a wife or mother. Focus on fixing you. Not trying to fix his pockets, 'cause if he doesn't have shit, your kids wont have it's a trickle down effect bitch!"

And I hung up the phone.

Now before you go writing me about being the dumbest bitch in the

The Final installment of the Kalico Jones Trilogy

4 Miles to Freedom

world, don't bother. Shortly thereafter Eric and I broke friendship. I haven't heard or seen him. And he has not reached out to anyone in my family other than to say, he and his wife were going to try to work it out. That was almost one year ago.

I wish them well.

4 Miles to Freedom

NO MORE DRAMA IN MY LIFE?

Now back to my Puerto Rican Prince...Mr. Mo...We were all over the place like I said, just hanging out enjoying each others company. And we would probably still be together if it weren't for Yonkers Raceway. Yonkers 10701 where I would be with Mo and members of my family enjoying a nice time at the slot machines.

"Hello, what will you be having this evening?"

It was a beautiful woman bartender asking me my choice of beverage. "Johnny Walker Black cut free with green hair" translation: I WANT THAT SHIT YOU'RE SIPPING ON. NOT THAT WATERED DOWN B.S. YOU'RE SERVING THE MASSES.

And I got just that. JW Black straight up with "green hair" aka lime.

So I'm in Yonkers Raceway running into folks I hadn't seen in years and Mo is getting a little bothered by it. I could tell because he kept looking at me with this expression on his face as though to say, "get away from my girl" as I was now his girlfriend and dating him exclusively.

Everyone is having fun. I am laughing and talking with my folks and the bar yells out "last call" I put in another drink order and ran to the rest room. While in the bathroom, I bumped into two more folks from my past and we started talking. Well I don't know how long we were in there, it must have been a long while because as we exited the restroom there were barriers set up so that you could only go outside. The place was officially closing and I couldn't get to my party. When I got outside I realized I left my cell phone in the bathroom. Ugh! No phone, I walked to a payphone, drunk...let me take that back I WAS ANIALATED. I WAS TORE UP FROM THE FLOOR UP AND

The Final installment of the Kalico Jones Trilogy   65

4 Miles to Freedom

SO MY RECOLLECTION IS A BIT FUZZY. Let's just say I ended up at a friend's house, where I made a few calls and got into a taxi. But BEFORE I got to my brother's house the taxi stand dispatcher attempted to fondle a very drunk me. YES, I'm going to put it right out there...I went to get a taxi in Mt. Vernon and the dispatcher fondled me as I tried to use the restroom in the place. Why? Because I was beyond drunk. So when they tell you "don't drive drunk, take a cab" I'm going to tell you...**DON'T GET DRUNK BECAUSE NOT ONLY ARE YOU UNABLE TO DRIVE BUT YOU ARE UNABLE TO FIGHT OFF SOMEONE ATTEMPTING TO DO HARM TO YOU.** So being drunk out in the street is a no no. and NO I didn't call the police. Well actually I did. I called the next day and was told I would have to come back to Mt. Vernon to file an incident report, but I refused.

I let my people handle it for me a few days later.

JUNIOR I know...you're sorry, right? Fuck you. It's your job to protect someone in that situation NOT take advantage.

Ok, so I get to my brother's house in New Rochelle and I crawled up next to my daughter and went to sleep. The next morning we were awakened by continuous calls from my mother, who was up all night trying to convince Mo I was at my brother's house asleep and not with another man. I immediately reached out to him and asked him to drive me back to Jersey. As we got closer to my place Mo asked me for my house key. He said he had to go to the bathroom. He took the key and ran in the house. We followed behind him but could not get in.

The door was locked.

We stood outside in the hallway for almost a half hour until Mo let us in. We banged on the door. We rang the doorbell, even yelling through the window, but for some reason, Mo did not let us in.

When we finally did get it, I sent my daughter to her room to watch a bit of television or read a book and I immediately went to the bathroom and turned on the shower, Mo was on his was out the door.

"What's the rush Babe?"

4 Miles to Freedom

"Nothing, I just have to get back home, my father asked me to do him a favor, so I can't stay."

"Well can you give me a few minutes to jump in and out the shower? You know I don't like Ivy in here by herself...I'll be quick." And I jumped into the shower to wash off whatever germs I picked up during Junior's infamous "fondle."

I came out of the bathroom and headed to my bedroom. Hold up... is that something red on my picture? What in the world... I walked over to one of my favorite pieces of art. It's a black girl looking up into darkness with a tear rolling down her cheek. I call that painting "Kj of the past" it's one i enjoy so much, that I purchased one for a dear friend after the untimely death of her mother.

I put my hand on the red stuff. Hold on. This looks like lipstick. I don't wear red lipstick. I touched it again, it was hard, but smooth. it was NAIL POLISH! I walked into my bedroom and looked around to find that ALL of my artwork had spots of RED nail polish on the glass and frames. EVERY last piece! But here's the funny thing; the polish appeared to have been put on and removed. Who would do such a thing.

I went in my closet to grab a nightgown and looked down to the floor to find a piece of paper with writing on it. I picked it up to read: "God takes care of babies and fools and you surely ain't a baby. Take care and don't fucking call me!" signed, MO.

MO! Mo?

What the f---?

I looked over to where Mo was sitting, on my bed, a little red in the face and visibly anxious...I lifted up the paper and said, "Sweetie, what's this?" as I tossed the paper in his direction.

"Oh don't pay that any attention. I wrote that last night when I thought you left me in Yonkers to go hang out with one of your ex boyfriends we ran into while gambling."

The Final installment of the Kalico Jones Trilogy

4 Miles to Freedom

"Hold on...you were in my house?"

Mo got up from the bed, "Yes, I came here because I didn't know what happened to you. I was nervous. I kept calling your cell phone. Your mom didn't call me back. Baby I was scared for you."

Not being able to get beyond this nigga being in my house, I asked him again, "Mo, you were in my house?"

He began to stutter and I began to yell. No he didn't pull and "Eric" on me. "What the fuck were you doing in my house?"

"Oh I guess its time for me to leave, you're cursing now and I don't want to hear that. If you want to know the truth...I thought you ditched me and so I came here to see who you were coming home with and what time you got in. After about an hour of you not answering your phone, I started calling your mother. I told her I thought you were lost."

"Nigga how does a person who grew up in Yonkers, get lost in Yonkers? Save that shit for someone else. HOW did you get in my house?"

Stretching out his arms to prevent me from slapping him, "Kali... Kali...Kali...Please do not yell, your daughter is in the other room. Please calm down. I came in through the window."

Not another mother fucker and my window! Damn first floor apartment 'cause my ass was too lazy to go to a higher floor with all the shopping I do...the bags would kill me. Let me just explain: My garden first floor apartment was on a busy street in the town i lived in...a BUSY street. And picture this apartment being on the first floor FACING the middle of a courtyard! Yes, you read it right, a courtyard! You walk into the development where there are seven buildings. Three on the right, three on the left and one in the back that connects the buildings on the right and left... and ALL the buildings, although they have separate entrances, all the buildings are CONNECTED...that means my neighbors in the next building who were on the first floor could hear me fucking if they were home. Apartments were just that close. And my apartment faced the middle

4 Miles to Freedom

of those buildings = the courtyard, where everyone entering or exiting these seven buildings had to walk by.

Damn these niggas really had GUTS!

I said to myself, "I bet nigga put the polish on my artwork." But I couldn't prove it. Since my WINDOW of "opportunity" appeared to be accessible to anyone with GUTS and I had a long list of men who were pissed with me for one reason or another, anyone could have done it.

Nah, I bet it was him.

I looked on my dresser for my red polish, it was open but not hard. That means, the polish had to have been opened recently. And I knew for a FACT it wasn't opened by me. I turned to Mo, "Did you use my red nail polish to deface my property?"

"I cleaned it off, so its not defacing."

I sucked my teeth and pointed to the door, "Please, get the fuck out." I didn't even look him in the face when I said it.

He turned in my direction half way down the hall and asked, "Can I at least say goodbye to your daughter?"

And in my loudest yell, "Nigga are you serious? Get the fuck out and lose my number Jackass!"

Mo has called me too many times to count since then. My job, my house, my cell...up until the day I got sick of him whining and I changed my number...Ooops I'm sorry, NUMBERS, I changed all of them: home, cell, etc.

The Final installment of the Kalico Jones Trilogy

4 Miles to Freedom

IN THE MEANTIME AND IN BETWEEN TIME IF YOU GO YOUR WAY I'LL GO MINE

I was trying to focus on being a parent. I got a call from my homie Hev...he just broke up with girlfriend number 6 and repossessed the puppy he purchased her in the process.

Ring...ring..

Ring...ring..

"Yeah what's up Hev, your God Daughter's tuition is due, are you..."

He interjected, "Does Ivy want a puppy?"

"What? You know I don't want nothing else in this house that needs to be fed Nigga, no...she doesn't NEED a puppy."

"Bring my little girl over here and get this dog, this bitch acted like a chicken head and so I told her to remove herself from the house, leave everything I paid for, including the dog."

Laughing, "Damn Hev...the dog? What did the dog do to you?"

"Just stop it with the jokes and get your ass over here quick with my baby so she can get this dog."

And we jumped in the car and headed to an undisclosed location in Jersey to pick up the cutest MaltiPoo I have ever seen. It was an apricot poodle mixed with a Maltese and gorgeous. The hair was

4 Miles to Freedom

beautiful. Hev came outside with the puppy, kneeled down in front of my daughter and said, "Here you go princess and you can name it whatever you like, it's a boy." And gave her a kiss on the forehead.

Seeing the way Hev interacted with my daughter gave me mixed emotions. I was hurt watching all my male homies step up and be there for my daughter. Even the local barbershops in my neighborhood supported my daughter. Each time she was selling something; Girl Scout cookies, Lotion...yes lotion was a fund raiser, books, etc. we could always depend on the guys at 3D barbershop in Montclair and all the other shops on that block to support my little one. Which made it such a shame neither her father nor his family took part.

"You mean he's mine?"

"Yep, he's yours sweetheart, just keep making God Daddy happy with those straight a's and that little lady disposition."

"Thank you God Daddy...thank you!" By this time Ivy was jumping up and down filled with excitement.

As for me, I was thinking, "Not another mouth to feed...damn!"

"So princess, what are you going to name him?"

"Uncle God Daddy, I'm going to call him Licorice."

And Ivy took Licorice by his leash and led him to the car. We returned home to a message from Hev.. "Take the dog to Animal Kingdom in East Orange this coming Tuesday, be there in the morning, I paid to have him groomed. Every three weeks, he goes back for grooming and tomorrow, go to Petco and get whatever you like, there is a five hundred dollar gift card at their West Orange, NJ location with your name on it Ivy. I love you."

Hev is quite the class act. But he's always been like that. He's been a part of my life with consistency throughout the years and truth be told, he's about the ONLY person from my past who I brought with me in my present and who will be with me in the future. He has Thanksgiving and Christmas with my Mom and family. My brothers

4 Miles to Freedom

love him. My daughter adores him and he is the person I would call if I ever needed anything. He's done tuition when I fell on hard times trying to move and get furniture, etc at the same time. He has and continues to take us out to dinner and lunch, although he will NOT buy any champagne or anything with alcohol in it for me after my DUI arrest.

BOOP BOOP...
THAT'S THE SOUND OF THE POLICE...

It had been a few weeks after Hev sprung the dog on us and almost one year after my letter to homeboy and we still have not heard a peep from him or his family. I was on my way to meet a group of friends at Richie Cecere's in Montclair, NJ when the police stopped me as I pulled into the parking lot.

Flashing lights, sirens and a loud command over a speaker, "Please stop your vehicle!...Please stop your vehicle."

What the fuck?

I pulled over on Walnut Street by the railroad tracks and opened the driver's side door to get out of the vehicle I was driving, which just happened to be three days old. A red Nissan courtesy of a Fireman who lived in the area. I opened the door and placed my foot out on the concrete, "Please stay in your vehicle...get back in the vehicle now!" guns drawn, I felt like I was in the wild wild west...I quickly took my hand off the door of the car and put my leg back in the vehicle. Just then two officers walked over, "Miss do you know why we stopped you?"

"No"

"Well it appears as though you ran the light back there on Grove & Walnut streets"

"It APPEARS or did I? The light was yellow and I went through it, since when did that become illegal?"

4 Miles to Freedom

"Ok, she's being sarcastic...Madam I need your license and registration card."

I looked in my purse and handed the officer my vehicle registration and driver's license.

"So you're from New York."

"Yep"

"Then why are you here?"

"I live here now."

"Really, for how long Mrs....Mrs....Jones"

"For about two years, why?"

"Well then you know you are responsible to turn your New York license in after you've lived in this state for 90 days."

"Nope, didn't know that and again, why am I being detained?" I rolled my eyes and sucked my teeth. I was pissed off and afraid my alter ego was going to kick in and my ass was going to end up in the Montclair town jail.

"Excuse me" and without even answering my question the officer took my license and registration card back to his patrol car to do what, I don't know exactly, my guess was to make sure the "black girl" from New York didn't have any warrants.

A few moments later, two more patrol cars showed up, sirens blazing and lights on, I was now cornered. I'm sitting there thinking, "Did I rob a bank and don't know it?" or better yet, "Did I have an outstanding warrant dating back to that shit with Kelly and didn't know it?" nah that was cleared up, right?

Right.

"Madam I'm going to ask that you get out of the car now."

4 Miles to Freedom

"For what may I ask."

"Nope, get your ass out of the car."

"Excuse me officer, there is no need to be rude here, I do have rights, I asked why I was being detained and you didn't respond and now I'm asking…"

"Listen Miss, we can do this here, or we can arrest you and do it down at the station."

I sucked my teeth and thought fuck it…I'd rather be at the station. I responded, "Officer, I'd rather not get out the car. I feel this is a hostile situation, you have been rude, please ask a female officer to handle me, thank you."

And the Officer, walked over to two female cops and said, "The bitch wants one of you to handle her…good because she's got some attitude on her and may have the potential to be disruptive or even combative."

The two female officers, who were WHITE, walked over to me. The smaller of the two WHITE female officers said, "Miss, please step out of the car." And I did just that. Legs first, hands on top of my head. I looked up to find myself surrounded by five squad cars and a host of folks, my new neighbors, who were coming home from work on the Montclair direct train line. I was so embarrassed.

"Miss we would like to search your vehicle, are you in possession of any drugs, or weapons?"

"No"

"No what…weapons, drugs…no what?"

"No you can't search my vehicle and right now I ask that you please take me to the nearest police station to finish this arrest."

The first officer, a WHITE MALE police officer walked back over and yelled in my face, "Did you hear anyone say you were being

The Final installment of the Kalico Jones Trilogy

4 Miles to Freedom

arrested?"

"No, but I am outside, hands on my head, surrounded by five squad cars, being asked permission to search my vehicle and not once, after I have complied with your request for my license and registration card have I been told why I am still here."

"Because you ran the light and upon approaching your car, I smelled marijuana."

I laughed, "Officer you are being ridiculous. I know it can't be that hard to make a ticket quota in Montclair. I do not do drugs officer, that's ridiculous, you know what...right now you can just take me to the fucking station." Yep, your girl was now cursing. This mother fucker tried to tell me I was high.

"Madam I would ask that you not use that tone" one of the female officers chimed in.

"Or what? You're going to arrest me for cursing. Fuck off. Resisting arrest...Can't happen. You see that group of professional women across the street and those two Township of Montclair Firemen, those are my friends. We were to meet here tonight right before you stopped me, I'm sure out of the seven of them, ONE of them is videotaping this entire thing with their cell phone, so fuck you! Arrest me!"

I guess my ass was loud because just then one of the people in my party – a fireman, came over and introduced himself, "Hi officers, I am Mr. Kenneth Banks with the township fire dept, this is a dear friend of mine, could you tell me what is going on?"

And the WHITE COP pulled my party, a BLACK fireman to the side and told him that he was doing a routine stop after noticing me run a red light and when he pulled me over I began to shout absurdities at him and appeared to be hostile, even combative... almost testing his authority. I yelled, "And don't forget to tell him how you said you smelled WEED in my fucking car prick!"

"Kali shut up!" my friend yelled.

4 Miles to Freedom

I put my head down and thought, I should spit on his ass when he walks back over here. WEED? What the fuck, he can't be serious. WEED. Thank goodness I was smart enough NOT to let him search my car, his ass probably would have planted something on me.

My friend came over to me, and said, "They're letting you go, but you will have a ticket for not having your license changed over to New Jersey and you will have another ticket for having temp tags two days beyond the expiration date."

I just shook my head. When the officer handed me the tickets, I mumbled, "That's why y'all always getting shot at."

And the cop whispered back, "I'll see you again nigga bitch."

I looked up at him and we made a strangest eye contact I've ever experienced to this day. The look in his eyes said more than that nigga bitch comment ever could. I knew…I was going to see his ass again.

But NOT this soon.

After telling the story of my Montclair police experience to everyone in the place who would listen, I decided I had enough = 7 glasses of Chianti, and would go home. I say this to you because I had plenty to eat and I did not FEEL as though I was "drunk" or even "tipsy." I said goodnight to my party, retrieved my car from valet parking and drove down Elm Street and around to Orange Road where the baby sitter lived. I was actually going to pick up my daughter prior to going home. I got out of the car and turned it off. I stood outside laughing and joking with friends and about ten to fifteen minutes into our conversation, four Montclair Police squad cars pulled up. I'm talking sirens blazing, lights, driving on the side walk and everything! There was one car in front of my car (which was OFF and parked). There was another cop car in the back of my car and one more on the side of my car…I was officially blocked in. I continued to talk with my folks only because I didn't think this entire production by the police department was about me…

A police officer came upon me, "Miss have you been drinking?"

The Final installment of the Kalico Jones Trilogy

4 Miles to Freedom

"Excuse me? And so what if I was? I'm not driving. I'm on the side walk what are you going to arrest me for, public intoxication?"

"Miss is that your car?"

"Yeah, and…"

"Then you are under arrest for DWI."

"What…I don't think so, you can't just do this…I know my rights, you can't do this."

And as soon as I began to plead my case the SAME officer who called me a "nigga bitch" right before he promised to see me again, made good on his promise, "Hi Miss Jones, we meet again…how about you walk this line for me, turn around and walk back and please keep your hands to your side straight out, and your feet must be heel toe, heel toe."

"Well it's good to see you too, but that is not going to happen officer, I am pigeon toed and my ankles are not designed that way. If I walked heel to toe, I will certainly lose my balance and fall, got any other bright ideas."

"Well walk the line however you wish."

And my ass did just that and was doing well with it too. Until I had to turn around. I leaned to the side and all of a sudden I was rushed by three cops who threw me up against my car, head first and damn near broke my arm trying to put handcuffs on me. I was beyond myself. I began to yell my mothers home telephone number out to one of the folks I was talking with right before this fiasco and was shouting all sorts of shit at the police officers, "Fuck you" "Die Slow" "I'm going to fuck your teenage sons and make their lives a mess"…just all sorts of shit. All the way down to the station.

When I arrived at the police station, I had no shoes on my feet. My Ann Taylor shoes were "missing" but my handbag was still with me despite having a full prescription of Xanax with the label torn off in it. So I'm in the Montclair police department screaming at the

4 Miles to Freedom

top of my lungs while my mother was in the process of finding out her daughter had FOUR outstanding warrants...all tickets in NJ that stemmed from parking. Did you know that in the state of New Jersey parking tickets turn into warrants? Neither did I.

I began to yell, "I gotta use the bathroom...I gotta use the bathroom!" as officers walked by the cell I was being CAGED in, hands cuffed behind my back with no shoes and no place to even sit. My ass was on the floor. I laid on the floor and cried. Then I laughed, then I prayed...then I shouted more curse words at the officers.

"Miss Jones, you have to stop this yelling if you want to go to the bathroom." A BLACK officer attempted to calm me down.

"This place is a fucking joke! The cop who arrested me called me a nigga bitch earlier and promised he would see me again, what did he do, wait for me to come out of Cecere's and follow me to arrest me for DWI..."

"I can't answer that, but I am going to just tell you something little sister, I need you to calm down so you can be safe. I get off soon and I am concerned about you. Don't give them anything else to charge you with."

"Well I have my period. Do you think they can give me a fucking tampon out of my purse and my medicine?"

"Don't be vulgar."

"Since when is a monthly period vulgar, BROTHER?"

"Ok. Let me see what I can do, but I need you to promise me you are going to behave, please sis...behave."

And just then I knew...HE didn't have to say it. HE knew that I would find myself in more trouble than I was already in if I didn't follow his advice and get a grip on my emotions. Someone came to unlock the door.

"Why thank you officer, do you think I can have my purse?"

The Final installment of the Kalico Jones Trilogy

4 Miles to Freedom

"No"

"Well I have to get a tampon out of it, can someone get it for me?"

"Use tissue."

I felt the bitch switch flick to the on position. "Are you denying me a sanitary napkin...are you saying I cannot have a tampon? Out of my OWN purse?"

"You want to act like an animal, we are going to treat you like an animal, use tissue."

And I was escorted, still in handcuffed, from the cell I was in, to another cell that had a toilet. There was a young white female in there complaining about how she wanted to know why she wasn't being let out after her grandfather posted bail on her behalf. I asked her to turn around, "Do you mind turning around while I use the bathroom honey?"

"Oh no, go ahead Ma, do you...but I don't think me looking on is going to matter with all these cops looking up your ass."

I turned around to see over six police officers watching me as I attempted to use the bathroom, on my period. It was horrifying. The officers laughed and pointed as I tried to whip my ass with hard tissue that had become half way wet and stained due to it being rolled on the floor in my direction because there was no toilet paper when I squatted over the toilet.

I looked up, "What...y'all never seen a black girl's pussy before?" and I guess that was too much to handle because one cop yelled, "Watch your fucking mouth!"

And that wasn't enough for me because I said, "I know every white man in here wants to know what my pussy feels like...and taste like."

The Sergeant came over and kicked in the door, "That's enough out

4 Miles to Freedom

of you, get your ass up. You're done!"

And two female officers went to handcuff me before I could even pull up my panties. And then to add to that, as I was being lifted off the toilet some sort of device was shoved in my face and I was asked to blow in it. I pulled my head back and said, "What is this?" and the Sergeant snatched it out of the female cop's hands and said, "Did you get that...the bitch just refused a breathalyzer."

BASTARDS!

Yep I said it.

They treated me like shit.

Four hours later, damn near five. My mother had paid over 1200 bucks to bail my ass out of jail which was really the total amount of parking tickets I had accumulated over the year plus I had lived in New Jersey...I had tickets in all the surrounding cities, it was a mess...but thank GOD for mom!

My daughter had been picked up from the sitter by my mother and she was in the lobby of the station sitting by her grandmother awaiting my release. I left the station under the cover of darkness, with no shoes, messy hair, wet clothing, FIVE court appearance tickets and...the media! My mother handed me a pair of sunglasses as I ran across Bloomfield Avenue barefoot to the town car my mother had waiting to take me and my daughter home.

I got in the back, "Mommy, I'm sorry for what I have done, but trust me it was not my fault, the same officer..."

"BITCH! I don't give a fuck about an officer, you got whatever you fucking deserved. I told you to get your ass out of Cecere's after the second glass of wine, but NO...you have to always prove you are the baddest bitch...always gotta show you are the head bitch... and that shit just cost me almost two grand and could have cost you your daughter had you not been arrested before you went upstairs to get her. So don't give me no stories about how the officer waited for you...I know he waited for you...YOU knew he was going to

The Final installment of the Kalico Jones Trilogy

4 Miles to Freedom

fuck with you and you still took your ass in and stayed, so deal with it Kali...just deal with it!"

"Mommy...I was not drunk. I was out of the car, I was talking, the car was off...how can I get a DUI and not be in the car?"

"I'm going to tell you like your brother Charlie told me, if they can prove you operated the vehicle from the bar to the sitter's house, that's DWI."

"But that's not fair."

"Life isn't fair. It isn't fair that your daughter is up at two in the morning sitting in a police station listening to her mother act like a fucking nut for hours...that's not fair."

"I'm sorry Ivy...Mommy loves you."

"I love you too mommy are you okay...grandma said they took our car." And they did too. The car was impounded and I had to get it in the morning. I got home, and went straight to bed.

The next day I arrived back at the police station for two reasons. I had woke up to severe bruises on my back, chest, throat area and legs, black and blue marks that were the direct result of a DWI arrest gone wrong. The cops used excessive force and it showed. The second reason was because the towing company had requested a police release of impound form in order for me to get the car.

I entered the police station, "Good morning, I want to get a release form for my car, I am Kali Jones."

The cop behind the glass left and came back with four more officers. "You're Miss Jones, we've been waiting for you" one of the officers said. I recognized him. He was the one who told me to "use tissue."

"Oh really, well do you think its possible for me to speak with someone about filing a civilian complaint?"

4 Miles to Freedom

"Sure" and he left the window. I stood in the lobby of the police department for twenty two minutes waiting for the office to return with my release form for the tow place and instructions on how to file a civilian complaint. But I would get one out of two because the sergeant, you know the one who called me a "nigga bitch" came to the front desk as I was showing my bruises to two BLACK officers and said, "Take this hold release and get the fuck outta here before I re-arrest you!" and threw the form at me.

WOW.

My ass hurried up and got out of there and filed a civilian complaint that following week, however that went unattended to. Translation: No one has gotten back to me yet.

In the mean time I hired an attorney who told me that a refusal to take a breathalyzer was considered "the kiss of death" in the state of New Jersey and that the best he would do his best to have all or most of the charges thrown out, but he was going to be unable to get a judge to consider dropping the DWI...So I would have to cop to a DWI and take a seven month hit to my license...Damn my ass could not afford to have a suspended license. And what about my insurance rate? I was pissed, but had no choice.

Three months and 1100 dollars in fines later, I had a DWI on my record and a seven month restriction on my license. We got to court and the cops who arrested me, ALL of them were there. This time I looked totally different. I had a long weave, full face make up and folks were recognizing me "Aren't you Kalico Jones, the author?" the police didn't know what they had on their hands. I get to the front of the court room and the judge asked me recite the chain of events that led up to my arrest. Where I was, how many glasses of wine I drank, etc. all things that didn't matter because they didn't affect the bottom line which was me, your girl, getting that damn DWI. "Miss Jones we are suspending your license for a period of seven months and fining you 1100 dollars, please turn in your license."

And just then my attorney interjects, "Your honor, we respect the sentence and agree, but my client's license is from another state and

4 Miles to Freedom

so you do not have the authority to suspend it, nor confiscate it."

The judge looked at the Prosecutor, as if to say, "Dog, you made this deal with her people BEFORE you did your homework." The cops all stood on the side lines visibly pissed. All this and the bitch is going to win in the end...

The judge turned back to me and said, "Miss Jones' since we can't suspend your license, we are going to put you on the unauthorized list, which means you cannot drive in the state of New Jersey for a term of seven months."

I hugged my attorney, got in my b-boy stance and bopped out of the court room, holding my crotch, like I was Mary J.

The next day my ass was back on the block where the arrest took place, in a low cut top with push up bra, tight jeans and heels ... BRAGGING ABOUT HOW THE POLICE COULDN'T STOP ME, got in my CAR and DROVE off.

Six months and Three weeks into my seven month suspension of driving privileges in the state of NJ, I got into a car accident and my car was totaled...IN NJ. That's what I get for being a smart ass. I called an ambulance to take me to the hospital at the scene, to prevent me from being arrested for driving on the revoked list. It worked.

So NO...Hev does not pay for champagne when we go out.

Thank GOD it wasn't a criminal offense, but it did hinder me from being able to get a job with a prominent accounting firm, once they saw the first couple of lines of the police report, that read:

FOUR outstanding warrants and listed the townships where the warrants were. NEVER did they say they were for unpaid parking tickets. FUCKERS.

AND so after trying my hand over and over again with the employment agencies...and being told NO because of the first line of that arrest report...I GOT TIRED OF EXPLAINING THAT SHIT,

4 Miles to Freedom

and decided to keep my ass out of corporate America for a while. I landed a new job at a University and it's been so far, so good. Thank you Jesus! And Jesus it is!

I left the BOYS alone and began to focus on my purpose in life and just being a good mother. I was doing well until...

DADDY WHO?

We heard from homeboy.

He was asking to see his daughter.

Ugh! What in the world did he expect me to say, "No?" I called him back and begged for consistency...and he promised just the same.

Too bad he didn't keep his promise to visit his daughter. And don't go crying for my child, because its not hardly that serious. Its not like SHE SAW HIM and THEN didn't keep the promise to be consistent...he DIDN'T show up, BUT he did keep his promise to be consistent. He consistently does not show up. He consistently does not call. And it's all good. WE consistently excel and strive to do better. We consistently try to not let that bother us or interfere with what we have going on as a family unit that is tight. We started going to Church. That's right...KJ even joined the mass choir at the Church we belong to and my daughter sings in the youth choir. We are active within our Church and I even teach Bible study to the teens when needed. I am the founder of a company that finds donations for organizations in need, such as women's shelters, etc. and its going great. I'm meeting a bunch of positive folks and I like the way my life is going right now. I promised myself I wouldn't do more than I could handle and so I'm coasting...

Ring...ring...

Ring...

"Thank you for calling the Kalico Jones project, how can I help you?"

"Hi Mrs. Jones please."

4 Miles to Freedom

"Speaking"

"Mrs. Jones, this is R&R properties, you are a resident at 111 Park Place"

"Yes, how can I help you?"

"I have in my possession an order for removal. You have a dog Maam and it has to leave the premises in three days or you will face eviction."

"I'm dog sitting" – LYING

"Maam three days"

"But the owner wont be back for five days."

"Ok Maam, five days or we will start eviction proceedings."

I put my head on my desk and began to cry. We've had Licorice for almost two years and my daughter was attached to him. They slept together. She would open the door and he would jump on her. It was a match made in heaven. What was I going to do? How could I break her heart by telling her the dog had to go. I called Pet hotels in the area. I was going to put him in a kennel until we found a new place, this way we could see him every day and have him when we found a new place, but they were too expensive. I called my mother, "Ma... the landlord called, Licorice has to go."

"Oh Kal...Ivy is going to be so sad. Oh my goodness what are we going to do?

"I don't know, I have five days to figure it out though. First I think I am going to see if I can find another apartment."

"I know you and Ivy love the dog sweetie, but to move to keep a dog when you just finished renovating this place is ridiculous," my mother was trying to sound as pleasant as she possibly could under the circumstances, honestly it sounded as though her voice was shaking.

The Final installment of the Kalico Jones Trilogy

4 Miles to Freedom

I was now beginning to sob aloud, "Ma, what am I going to do…this little girl's heart is going to break…I have to break her heart…"

"Kal first you have to calm down, and second you have to think of a plan, call Brandon…ask him about the guy who came over and Licorice took a liking to him immediately…what's his name?"

"Tony…yeah, Licorice did like him and I know he has a nice big house and yard…The dog would be taken care of…let me reach out to Brandon." I hung up.

Dag, I forgot all about Tony, Brandon's best friend. He came over to my apartment a few weeks back to check on the wiring for my telephone. I had some work done and the construction workers cut a main wire which resulted in static on the lines. Tony had come over to fix it as a favor to my neighbor Brandon, a guy who I have to tell you was great with my daughter and kids in general. He would walk up to the neighborhood kids and say say, "Hey, if you can count the money in my hand, you can have it." And even if they were wrong, he would still give them the money. Brandon and I dated for a little while, but my need to be "seen" by the masses was a bit much for his reserved lifestyle. We are still pretty decent friends and who knows…we may end up together one day down the road…Once I free myself to allow someone to love me and my daughter without thinking they may leave when they realize I am a woman who is hurting.

I closed the door to my office and called Brandon. He was at work. "Hey Baby…I need to talk with you, got a minute?"

"KJ can this wait until later and we talk when I get home?"

"I don't think so, its about Ivy"

"Ok whatcha need?"

"Brandon, the rental office called my job, Licorice has to go."

"Man…Ivy is going to be upset. That little girl is going to cry herself into a frenzy."

4 Miles to Freedom

"I know...I know and I've been here on the job crying about how I am going to tell her and how this is going to affect my household because I don't think a trip to toys r us is going to deprogram her from this. I just don't see that working for this situation."

"I told you to stop doing that last year when homeboy didn't show up for the umpteenth time...you cant keep giving her stuff to blanket her pain...she has to be able to feel Kali...don't let her be like you."

"What are you talking about...I feel."

"No you don't. You are a woman without EMOTION, unless it involves your daughter, that's why me and you are not together now."

"Oh, so this conversation is no longer about Licorice needing a place to live."

"What do you want me to do? You must have had something in mind when you called me."

"Can you ask Tony if he would be interested in adopting Licorice? He came to mind because of the way Licorice took to him when he came in the house."

"Yeah, 'cause anybody that crazy dog likes...."

"Shut up...just ask him for me please and I will see you at the house later. Do you know what you want for dinner?"

"So you back cooking for me now? You're a funny lady. Fix whatever, and I will see you around six."

And I left the job, stopped by the supermarket, picked up my daughter and headed home.

"Mommy what's wrong?"

I looked at ivy, how could she tell something was bothering me?, "I just got a little bad news today and I don't know how to tell you."

The Final installment of the Kalico Jones Trilogy

4 Miles to Freedom

"Mommy I'm a big girl...you can tell me anything."

"Ivy, the landlord said that Licorice has to go, we can't have any pets."

"No mommy I cant live without Licorice...he sleeps with me."

"I know baby, but what can we do? We have to find some place for him to go."

"Lets ask Daddy to take him."

"What?"

"Can I ask Daddy if he could take him?"

"You can do whatever you like Weenie...we'll call him after diner."

And after dinner Ivy called her father. It went to voicemail, "Daddy Hi its me, Ivy...I'm calling you to see if you could do me and mommy a favor and keep my dog while we look for a new place to live that will allow us to have Licorice. Our place now says we cant have him and I love him. Daddy please call me back."

She placed that same call, leaving that same message 18 times over the course of four days and homeboy never called back. Not even to say he couldn't do it. I tried to explain his behavior away by telling her that her "Dad" was working and probably didn't get the message, even almost insinuating that maybe she was calling the wrong number or not pressing the right buttons, but the outgoing voice message DID have his voice and so that didn't work.

In the meantime our one adoption "candidate" was on vacation and unreachable until the very last day...I had gotten a follow up call from the rental office reminding me that someone would be on the property to inspect my residence in two days and between those things and my search for an apartment that would allow pets...things were going no where FAST.

Buzzz....Buzzzzzzzz

4 Miles to Freedom

Who in the world is ringing our bell this time of day? It was 8:45 on a Sunday morning and since we weren't going to church, we were sleeping in.

Buzzzzzzzzzz.....Buzzzzz

Dag, someone must know we are home. I got up and answered the door. It was Brandon and Tony...I yelled, "Hold on...let me put on some clothes!" I raced back to my bedroom and found a pair of old long johns and threw them on under my nightgown and headed for the door. "Shhh, Ivy is still sleep."

"So Kal I was telling Tone that you wanted to know if he wanted to adopt Licorice and he said yeah."

"Please have a seat. The reason why we chose you to take the dog is because of the way Licorice interacted with you when you came by. If you are interested, we do have a few requests."

"Okay, I'm listening, shoot," Tony replied.

"You cannot change his name. You have to keep in contact with us. In the event you no longer wish to care for the dog, you have to return him to us AND..."

"You mean there's more...Brandon, you were right, she's a handful"

I hit Brandon, "AND...you have to allow Ivy to visit the dog...OH and you have to sign a contract that says all these things."

"Okay, so where is he?"

"You can't take him today. You can take him tomorrow. I want to just work with Ivy today and let her know today would be her last day with the dog."

"Ok sounds good."

And I'm telling you...it was just as if Licorice could hear us talking about him and knew what we were talking about...because just as

The Final installment of the Kalico Jones Trilogy

4 Miles to Freedom

Tony and Brandon were leaving...he ran into the living room and humped Tony's leg.

The next day, I sat on my sofa and watched my daughter cry hysterically as Tony signed the adoption papers for Licorice...to this day Brandon says his heart still breaks every time he thinks about it.

A few weeks into Licorice being out of the house, we found a new place. It was a grand residence not too far from where we were living, with a pool, gym, sauna, doorman, 24hr concierge service, etc...we were going to take the place SIGHT UNSEEN due to its premier location.

I took yet another hard look at homeboy's no shows / no calls and changed all the numbers. I kept telling myself I would move on and not give anyone associated with him a number to find us...and since we were moving...there would be no address for him to locate us either.

And since his name is not on my daughter's birth certificate...this trip out of the country would go uncontested...

4 Miles to Freedom

PASSPORT PLEASE

Essex County, NJ and we found the only passport office that stayed open late two days a week. My brother and mom were flying the family out to Jamaica for the weekend.

"I'm sorry Miss...you have all the proper paperwork, but you are missing the notice of consensus signed by the father parent allowing you to obtain a passport so the child can leave the country."

"I beg your pardon?" I was talking with a pecan colored woman who in every sense of the word was a BEAUTIFUL Black woman.

"You have everything filled out properly and I can still process YOUR passport application, but the child's application cannot be processed without a signed notice from the father consenting to out of country travel."

"Really, why is that? His name isn't even on the birth certificate."

"Do you have it, let me see please."

And I handed over the ONE document that up until that very moment was not a document I was proud to show. Who really wants to show their child's birth certificate with the NAME OF FATHER PART...BLANK? Exactly, no one. At least that's what I had been feeling through these years, up until the moment the woman in the passport office said, "Oh, sorry, we do not require the notice when the birth certificate is blank under that portion. When are you leaving the country?"

"We plan to leave in two weeks, I know this is short notice, can I pay to speed up the process?"

The Final installment of the Kalico Jones Trilogy

4 Miles to Freedom

"Yes, you would need priority processing and its costly but that is the only way you will be able to leave the country in two weeks."

And I paid $93 bucks extra per application to ensure we would have our passports on time to go.

4 Miles to Freedom

I'M RUNNING AS FAST AS I CAN BUT MY PAST... IT JUST KEEPS CATCHING UP TO ME

Ring...

Ring ...ring.

I opened my eyes, and tried to get my mind together. What time is it? I thought to myself, as I looked around to notice I had fallen asleep on my sofa, fully dressed in my work clothing and Freddie Fekkai hair. Damn, I don't remember if I ate dinner. I do know that after the third glass of "wind down" champagne, I did kick off my shoes and put my feet up.

Ring...ring...

Ring...

The phone was still ringing. I guess the three rings...four tops rule didn't apply to whomever was calling this time of night. I answer the phone, "Hello"

"You sound so sexy Ma"

"Who is this? And why are you bored at 3am?"

"Its Kevin...You got company? I wanna see you."

"Now you know I don't play that company shit during the week and especially when my daughter is home, what's up. You okay?"

"I miss you Ma. You got me feeling like I cant think."

The Final installment of the Kalico Jones Trilogy

4 Miles to Freedom

I was silent. Oh LAWD don't tell me I'm about to hear the "I love you KJ song" He continued, "So you have nothing to say?...You ain't fucking with me no more?"

"Kevin, I think you're nice and all but right now I'm at a place in my life where I don't want to be ninth inning pussy...I'm tired of that. I'm sick of being a cheerleader to men who claim they cant live without me, and then go off and marry other women. I told you that if and when you want to have a serious relationship, call me."

"Oh so I love you and I cant think ain't serious now?"

"I'm not saying it ain't serious. I mean I believe its serious to you... but what I am saying is that its NOT enough."

"I need you ma."

"NO you need some pussy. (sucking my teeth and exhaling) Kevin I have to go now, its after 3am and I have to not only get up and get myself together for work in three hours, but I have to get the kid together too. Call me when you are serious about me."

"What do you mean by that?" Kevin's tone was becoming increasingly loud, "What you mean by that Kali...when I'm serious about you? I have given you everything you've asked for. The new place, the car, the kids tuition, those 800 dollar suits you like to be in to let the chicks in your office know you don't need to be there, the shoes... what do you mean I'm not serious."

"Kevin, I'm talking about TIME. I want someone who is going to hold my hand. Take me out to dinner. Vacation, someone who cant live without me...minus the sex...minus the head."

"I take you out. I give you my time. I cant take you on vacation because of..."

I interjected, "Because of your GIRL, say it...say it"

"But I SEND you wherever you want to go, each time you want to jump up and take your little weekenders here and there...when

4 Miles to Freedom

one of your other dudes piss you off and you want to change your numbers and get missing...that's my money. And now you wanna throw Nadine in my face...I'm only with her because she has a lot of my stuff in her name, we don't even sleep in the same room. I'm not even sleeping with her."

"Whatever!"

Now I'm sitting up on my sofa, I'm in my b-boy stance, my swagger is setting in, that Madam Badness, The Infamous K to da Jizzay and I'm about to go in...He's on the phone yelling now. I don't know where homie is doing all this yelling at almost 3:30 in the morning. Bu my ass gotta go to work. My adrenalin is flowing, I'm tired, pissed and anxious all at once. I didn't get the chance to sleep off the champagne I had before I plopped my behind on the couch without taking off my very expensive suit, and this nigga is breaking all the rules with this call and his conversation, "Kevin, I told you when we first started out that I move like a dude. You asked me what that meant I told you it simply means I can love you today and kiss the ground you walk on and you do one little thing to me and I WILL forget you tomorrow. It meant that when its over, and you're searching for your boxers, I will be washed, prepped, fully dressed and damn near out the door. It means I'm a single woman who is doing her and making my way and I cannot, nor will I continue to commit myself to men who are in relationships. Period and I thought WE understood that and were in agreement....why are you changing on me Captain? What's going on with you? You're making me nervous."

"I love you Ma, I cant breath. I cant even look at this Bitch. I need you."

"Oh no...Don't go calling her a bitch now. You know I don't respect that type of shit, 'cause if you call her a bitch today you'll call me one tomorrow."

"I would never call you a bitch. I would call you MRS. NIGGA!" AND HE HUNG UP ON ME.

WOW...MRS. NIGGA.

The Final installment of the Kalico Jones Trilogy

4 Miles to Freedom

I'll TAKE THAT AS A COMPLIMENT.

I guess my no shows and refusal to accept gifts and calls from Kevin was beginning to bother him. But I had begun a new life. I wanted to walk with the very person who will never leave nor forsake me... GOD. I recommitted myself to MYSELF and I'm feeling good about my decision.

THE HOLY WHAT?

I can't tell you the exact time, but I can tell you the date, May 4th. I went up to the Altar to ask for prayer. I wanted to ask God for a very special prayer, I needed God to deliver me from myself. Strange request on the surface, but relevant to where I was in life and where I sit today as I write this. I stand in need of God's mercy, through unprotected sex, alcohol, and gluttony...YES, I stand in need of DIVINE mercy. I was doing well with the drinking. My champagne "habit" had slowed down and I appeared to have it going on, but that was only on the surface, because each time I heard something about homeboy, my ass picked up a drink. Each time my daughter came home and told me how she had a good time with my brothers – who have been acting more like fathers, I had a drink. Every time one of my "friends" showed my daughter any kind of love...you guessed it, I picked up a drink. I even started those late night cigarettes again.

It was like I didn't care about myself. Each time something I couldn't control occurred, I would lose all train of thought and find myself doing something I basically had no business...so yeah, I was asking God to clean house!

I got up and went to the Altar, standing there eyes filled with tears, and I looked to my right and there was Ruby, she was holding my hand as the Bishop walked in my direction. I stood there, looked him straight in the face and saw myself. Have you ever looked at a person and saw yourself? Well I did. I saw my stories, all of them, in this Man of God. He made a cross sign on my forehead with Holy Oil, grabbed me by the back of my neck with the other hand and began to pray. My hands still by my side, right hand held by one of my girlfriends and the left hand free, or so I thought, because a few seconds into the Altar Call, I felt something small and cold touch my hand. I looked down and it was my daughter. She smiled at me and said, "Mommy Jesus

4 Miles to Freedom

loves you." And right there, in that Church, On May 4th I was visited by the Holy Spirit. I am telling you this because I know some of you reading this may not believe in the existence of this entity... but I can tell you...ME, Kalico Jones, whore, slut, promiscuous, cocaine addict, countless abortions, drug dealer, drinking problem...ME...that chick, I can tell you first hand GOD does exist and HE was waiting for me all this time, which makes my current situation stupid. I slept with someone a few weeks ago, unprotected and I'm very upset with myself. An EX ...and he is an EX for a reason. My girlfriend Tawana told me to stop kicking myself and dust my life off and continue my walk and I did just that. But not before I spoke with my Aunt V..

It was her birthday and she sent me her telephone number, and I hadn't spoken with her since my little sister Ty's baby shower a few months prior.

After my Holy Ghost experience, I felt different, and although I had screwed up recently, my mistakes were no match for Jesus. I called my Aunt V who would prove that to be true.

Ring...ring...

"Hi Aunt V...Happy Birthday...its Kali!"

"Hey niecey niece (that's what she calls me), so your father told me you got the Holy Ghost, I'm happy for you...doesn't it feel good?"

And I told my Aunt V the very same thing I shared with you. Unprotected sex. Drinking. Etc. and she said, "Oh no niecey niece...please tell me you are not sharing this with others?"

"Well I was going to tell the Pastor and one of the Prayer Warriors at the Church."

"No you are not. You are going to pray to God for yourself. You do not have to tell your business to people, it's between you and God. You talk to God...YOU tell HIM what is going on. Repent and move forward."

"But I feel bad."

4 Miles to Freedom

"That's because your life is different now and so yes, you are going to feel convicted. But you have to repent, forgive yourself and move on….do you hear me?"

"Yes"

"And don't be running around telling your business to folks…learn how to keep your business to yourself."

"Ok…Well I know you have to go, I hear your other line ringing… I'm sure that's someone in the family trying to get through to wish you a happy birthday."

"Yes, but I want you to call me back if you need to, okay?"

"Yes"

"I love you niecey niece…you're gonna be okay."

"I love you too…thanks for the talk."

I hung up the phone and made a promise to regain control over my life by making better decisions. In the months following my life would begin to take shape. I started The Kalico Jones Project and was beginning to make my way through the political and community circuit in Essex County, NJ. My daughter's book "The Dinosaur and Silva" is doing great and she is working on her next book and continues to excel in school.

We were on our way to North Carolina to visit my Father and Step Mom when we got a call from homeboy's mother.

4 Miles to Freedom

GRANNY WHO?

She said she was in town and wanted to have a quick visit with her granddaughter...a little girl she hasn't seen since she was 2 or 3 yrs old. But although she hasn't seen her in years, she did know how she looked because we've sent photos. "I'm so sorry, we are on our way to the South, I have a few meetings and Ivy has a book signing."

"A book signing..."

"Yeah, your son didn't tell you she wrote a book?"

"No he did not."

"Wow, well yes, she's an author and doing quite well, we even mailed him and your father a copy."

"My father has a copy of her book?...No one told me."

"Oh I'm sorry to hear that."

"Well I want one autographed."

"We don't carry books with us, I would just go online to find it if I were you."

"Well send me the information so I can buy a few copies, I'm so proud of my grandbaby...that's wonderful!"

"Ok well thanks for calling. Take care," I hung up the phone and started packing for our trip to the Carolinas.

My father came to pick us up, he enjoyed the open road and fresh air

4 Miles to Freedom

the trip up Interstate 95 afforded him. He had all his favorite road side restaurants and knew the best places to get gas at cheap prices. He arrived at my place about 1am.

Telephone ringing

Ring….call from Concierge's desk…ring…

Call from Concierge's desk…ring…ring…

I had a cordless phone with talking caller i.d. I was going to make sure I knew who was on the other end of the phone prior to picking it up. Half asleep, "Hey Mo Deezy, what's good?" It was my doorman, I called him Mo Deezy just to break up the monotony he was used to from the other building residents."

"Hey Meena, your dad is here to get you and baby girl, you ready?"

"Yeah"

"Ok well y'all have a good trip and I'll let Miss D know you are out of town."

"Thanks Mo Deezy and you have a good week too…try not to miss us."

Miss D was the building manger and a person who people didn't play around with. She was about business and didn't feel the need to break bread aka make friends with no one. I admired that about her. Mo Deezy on the other hand…he was quite the people person, sometimes going out of his way to be friendly, Mo was my type of dude. Ahh, was actually going to miss him.

I opened the door to see my dad looking like he was on his second wind…"Hi Daddy!"

"Grandpaaaaaaaaaaaaaaaaaaa!"Ivy ran to my father and jumped so he could pick her up.

"How's grandpa's baby?"

The Final installment of the Kalico Jones Trilogy

4 Miles to Freedom

"Good"

"Y'all ready to rock and roll?"

"Yep"

"Well let's roll then"

And nine hours later, we were in North Carolina. My father had driven twenty straight hours and didn't complain about it once! My non driving ass, sitting in the backseat with my daughter, laughing and talking and sleeping on and off for nine hours of open road…Yippee!!

When we arrived to my dad's house, my step mom greeted us at the door, "Hey Kj, Ivy's grandmother called here, she left a message, make sure you call her back this morning."

"Ok." And I made my way to the telephone.

Ring…ring…

"Hi, this is Kj…Ivy's mom returning your call."

"Yes, how long are you guys going to be in the south?"

"One week, maybe five days…I don't know yet."

"'Cause I wanted to see my grandbaby…I haven't seen her in so long."

"Well I know we have a few things planned, but whenever you are in the area, you can just come on through, it doesn't matter, we can change stuff around."

"Oh that's nice of you, but I wouldn't want you to do that. I will call you tomorrow with a meet time."

"Sounds good to me." And it went on like this…that same raggedy ass conversation each day…for six days…up until and including the morning we were set to leave for home. This time I put Ivy on the

4 Miles to Freedom

phone...shit if she was going to lie about meeting again...she would have to do it directly to her grandchild.

"Hi Granny...am I going to see you?"

"Oh no pumpkin, its raining out here and there is flooding, I don't think I'm going to be able to make it."

"Oh that's too bad, maybe next time."

"Yes, maybe next time your mommy will bring you to MY house."

Can you believe that? She was trying to flip the script and blame her not seeing her granddaughter on me! Hell to da NAW...I took the phone, "We're getting ready to hit the highway, so we'll chat with you soon, take care of yourself." And I didn't even wait for her to respond. I gently placed the phone on the receiver...yes, I hung up on her ass. You know why? Because for six days she told me the same story about how she was running around doing things...things that I felt should have been placed on the back burner for two hours so she could see a grandchild of whom she has not seen in years. For six days I felt she not only played my daughter, but she burned up my cell phone minutes being deceptive when she knew she had no intention seeing the child. Now this is where I call her out her name, but I am not going to do it. This is where I tell you that if I were the OLD KJ, before my visit from yours truly, THE HOLY SPIRIT...I would be cursing and promising to see her in the street for playing my baby out like that, but I am not.

Granny who?

4 Miles to Freedom

DUNK ME TWICE!

It was Church, Church and more Church, as me and my little one began to settle in among the congregation. I was asked to teach Bible study to the teens in the Church and my daughter was singing her little heart out on the youth choir...we were happy, and life was better than ever.

"If there is anyone here who wants to be baptized today, please come forward." It was my Bishop Mr. Hobbs, doing the Sunday morning altar call on a TUESDAY! I was at Bible Study and I just felt as though the Lord was talking to me. HE was telling me that HE has anointed me to do GREAT works, but I had to be reborn...I just finished teaching my teen group when Sister Mathis came in my direction.

"Hi Ma..."Everyone called her that because she is the Church mother, "I want to be baptized this Sunday."

"Why not right now? Sunday might not come."

"Ok then, right now."

And I was led up to the room where I would be reborn in the Spirit that is Christ Jesus and my sins would be left in the water. I needed to feel that. I wanted to be closer to God. My Bishop called me to the front of the Church and put his arm around me and spoke to the congregation, "Now I know this young lady's testimony and she and I have some of the same stories, that's why I can relate to her. She has been active in the Church, her daughter is on the choir and this young woman is a child of God...I see great things in her...and today she is going to be baptized." and I changed into all white garments and was laid down in the water. I got up shouting! "Thank you Jesus, Thank you God" I was crying, but it wasn't a bad cry... it was a GRATEFUL cry. It was a "Thank you Jesus for your MERCY" cry.

4 Miles to Freedom

Because I witnessed my OWN funeral. The death of the old and the birth of the NEW...and everyone was shouting and hugging me and it was beautiful. My daughter was crying and laughing and smiling all at the same time, she hugged me and said, "Mommy God is proud of you!" and gave me a kiss on the lips. My daughter...I'm telling you she saved my life!

Miss Byrd, the "nanny" was there and she was very excited for me. Her and I have a great relationship, she is one of the few folks in my new place of residence who I have genuine love for. Between her and Heather, who gives me great decorating tips AND G. James, who give me great parenting advice, and advice in general, Suez and Miss D – the building manager...I believe I am in good hands. So between Church and a few good friends, my move to New Jersey is shaping up to be a great experience.

LET'S GET TOGETHER AND FEEL ALL RIGHT...ONE LOVE...COME TO JAMAICA AND FEEL ALL RIGHT!

(Singing) "Now I ...had the time of my life...and I owe it all to you..."

Can someone say "Montego Bay?" We were on the 2:40pm flight to Jamaica out of Newark International airport. Our scheduled arrival time would put us there just in time for a quick bite to eat and the beginning of the night life. Me, my brother Charlie, my daughter and my mom were all on the same flight. Now usually when we do family travels, we split up to ensure that in the event of a tragic situation, there are adults and children left to care for each other and carry on the family name...My brother and his wife fly this way all the time and suggested it to the family on this trip, which would change all of our lives.

"Charlie, I'm nervous, I have never been on a flight longer than one hour, my stomach is in knots, any suggestions?"

My brother Charlie is an international world traveler and so the sky is like the sidewalk to him. He summoned a flight attendant, "Excuse me, but my sister here is a little nervous so I'm going to show her how to fly the friendly skies...give her two shots of Jack Daniels and a bottle of ting...every time you see her glass getting empty...give her another and bring me the bill...thanks sweetie."

The flight attendant walked to the back of the place to fulfill his request all red faced from blushing...We could hear her telling the other flight attendants, "He called me sweetie" My brother Charlie has this thing within him. I cant explain it, but he is quite the charmer. EVERYONE

4 Miles to Freedom

loves this guy. He knows how to hang with the best of them and I finally figured out why he can with the best of them...BECAUSE HE IS ONE OF THEM...straight no chaser, by the time this book hits the printer, he should have the letters PhD following his last name. I'm proud of him. My brother Joey is no slouch either. He's got a management position within a well known financial institution and he's all over the place as well. Excelling in anything he sets out to do, I am happy to have such wonderful brothers and both of them are like fathers to my daughter.

"Hey you go Miss, two shots of Jack Daniels and a Ting chaser."

"Thank you...but I have to go to the bathroom, my nerves are shot... do you think you could walk with me?" I asked the flight attendant.

"Of course, no problem..." And she explained to me how the sky is safer than the highway and how until SHE gets worried, there was NO reason for me to worry because if is a problem, she would be the first to know about it. I returned to my seat to find that my mother had drank one of my shots of Jack.

It was a great flight and when we exited the plane, we had the opportunity to meet the Captain...A BLACK WOMAN! I KNOW MARTIN LUTHER KING JR. IS PROUD..WE'VE MADE GREAT ADVANCES...US BLACK FOLKS.

The weather in Jamaica was awesome. Me and my brother Charlie decided to ditch the rest of the family and hit the hip strip...we had a great time. We arrived back at the hotel when the sun came up, got about two hours of sleep, hit the hotel lobby for complimentary breakfast – THANKS RITZ CARLTON...and hit the beach for tans. After a few hours of sunbathing it was back to the hip strip, as we were leaving in the morning. We had a family weekender and our flight was leaving 8:50am Sunday morning. We would be back in Jersey in time for me and Ivy to attend Church!

We arrived home to a ringing telephone.

I turned to Ivy, "Who knows we're home?"

The Final installment of the Kalico Jones Trilogy

4 Miles to Freedom

"I don't know mommy, but don't get it."

"It may be an emergency, let me look at the caller i.d." It was homeboys mother calling our house...I picked up the phone, "Good morning to you, how are things?"

"I just got my grandbaby's books in the mail, God bless her little heart, the story is beautiful I am so proud."

"Thank you"

"You are dong such a good job with her, no thank YOU!"

"Would you like to speak with her?"

"Do you mind?"

I felt like saying, "Of course I mind...what the fu--- are you calling here for anyway...'cause she wrote a book? It ain't like y'all really care..." but I was SAVED now by the core definition of the word... and so KJ doesn't rock like that any longer. God had stepped in and I had to allow him ROOM to grow me up! I passed the phone to my daughter, "Hi Granny!"

"Hi honey, I read your book, its great ...you made that story up by yourself?"

"Yep, now I'm a writer like my mommy."

"Yes you are, but don't write the books mommy writes, okay?"

"Mommy writes good books, people love her."

"I don't doubt that...so are you going to sing in church today?"

"I don't know if we are going to church, we just got off the plane."

"You did?"

"Yep we went to Jamaica for the weekend, Uncle Joey and my grandma

4 Miles to Freedom

and uncle Charlie took us...it was fun!"

"You have a passport?"

"Yep and it has stamps on it too!"

I grabbed the phone from Ivy...no she was NOT questioning a 7 year old. "Hey its me on the phone, Ivy has to get ready for Church and I know you do too, we'll call you some time this week."

"Kali, I know its none of my business, but does my son know you took his daughter out of the country?"

"No, and I don't have to tell him. His name is not on her birth certificate, I have sole physical / legal custody of Ivy, I don't need his permission."

"You didn't think he should have known, in case of an emergency?"

The Final installment of the Kalico Jones Trilogy

4 Miles to Freedom

FLICK! There goes that BITCH SWITCH

"No, I didn't. Listen, can we just be honest here for a moment? Your son is the last person I would reach out to in the event of an emergency. I called him to ask for his information for the school contact sheet and he told me no."

"But one thing has nothing to do with the other."

"He didn't ask my permission when he took Kelly and her kids to Disney world. He didn't ask my permission or notify me when he purchased puppies for Mrs. Mattress tester from Hempstead, LI, but he couldn't return one call to his daughter to keep her puppy from having to be given away...so again...NO I didn't think my daughter taking a trip was any of his business."

"Ok well I'm going to stay out of it, I see you are getting upset...well y'all go on ahead to church...have a blessed day."

"You too. Take care of yourself."

And that...that was the last time I spoke with homeboy's mother.

HI HATERS?

Since the day they pulled me up out of that water...I've been feeling as though I am "bobbing and weaving" and I'm not talking about my head full of tracks! I'm talking about me ducking and dodging around people, places and things. I'm talking about folks popping back in my life from 1992 and people mistaking me for that chick they USED to know. I didn't know how to shake myself loose from the bullshit, and in my quest to become this NEW and IMPROVED person, my patience has been tested time and time again. My family, my friends, associates and just recently a person of whom I never thought I would not be speaking to.

Oh well. I learned in looking back through these books...that I have grown tremendously and I thank God for sustaining me...maintaining me and ORDAINING me to do HIS work. Too bad some folks wouldn't let the old KJ die.

Ring...ring...

"Yeah, what's up girl"

"Bitch that's why you a crack head...fuck you and I don't give a fuck who you are, when I catch you and beating your ass bitch?"

And she hung up the phone. Notice how I answered "What's up girl" that's because I knew the caller. She was a dear friend of mine or so I thought until she shared my business with someone who repeated it to me. I should have known this person was going to be an issue in my life eventually because every thing I was doing...SHE was doing. She surrounded herself with situations that were recipes for disaster and chaos...I introduced her to my circle of friends and she latched on to them like a shark. Each time I would introduce

4 Miles to Freedom

her to someone...she would make it a point to befriend them in some kind of way...and her and I not speaking did not stop her. What you see is the total opposite of what you get when dealing with folks who are imitators and I learned that from her the hard way...but I thank her because she taught me the real meaning of friendship.

I'm not going to go any further than to say, AFTER my baptism, I realized I had to remove a few folks out of my life and to be honest, and to keep it real with you...I was struggling with HOW to remove them. I knew they had to go...but I just didn't know HOW I was going to shake them off...As weeks turned into months...I guess GOD said, "She ain't doing it, so I'm going to do it for her." And this person's husband cursed me out! Just called me out of the blue and said, "My wife needs a break from you." And hung up. WHY? Because his wife shared something with HIM that I told her... something so very personal about myself that if someone repeated the same thing about YOU...You would flip. Then after that, my other "friend" called me and said, "Jones, I am so mad with you for not lending me that $500 dollars when I needed it. I realized you are not a true friend, because if you needed it, I would have done that favor for you, I'm not fuckin' with you no more!" and she slammed the phone down.

She wanted me to lend her 500 dollars after lending her 1000 dollars for back rent, another 200 dollars so she could take her kids school shopping. 100 dollars for car insurance, etc...And she is pissed with me to the point where she ended our friendship. I see...as long as I was her personal rent subsidizer slash ATM we were good. Then... there was the thing with two of my sisters, that I will not mention, just know that it was one thing after another after another after another since the Deacon from my church pulled me up out of that water.

God was attempting to wake me from my slumber. I had slept on so many folks to the point where I had someone say to me just recently after having a few glasses of wine – I did not drink – "Can I borrow a couple of dollars?" I said, "Girl I don't have any cash on me" and she replied, "I don't like you when you're not drinking... she removed her purse from my dinning table and left. Some times

4 Miles to Freedom

all you have to do is sit still and folks will remove themselves out of your life and you wont have to do one thing.

4 Miles to Freedom

KEEP SMILING... KNOWING YOU CAN ALWAYS COUNT ON ME... FOR SURE

It was homeboy's birthday and I was feeling a bit down. I picked up the phone so my daughter could call her father for his Birthday and the number had been changed. I took that time to sit down and really take stock of the events of just recent; fake friends and falling outs seemed to surround me on a daily basis...I decided to reach out to my cousin L.A.:

From: Kalico Jones

Date: Thursday, September 5, 2008 10:50 am

Subject: ugh!

To: yolanda@whereversheis.net

Lala I want to just share something with you for a minute because you are the ONLY person I trust with saying what I've been going through. I feel as though I am "back sliding" on some key things and I am really upset with myself right now. I've been crying a lot lately and real talk right now as I am typing this, I'm upset. I haven't been to Church in two weeks and my drinking has returned.

But don't worry, I'm not any where near where I once was with that, but I have had a few drinks over the past week or so. I really ask that YOU pray for me. Thanks. And tell God I need mercy on a screw up. I really need this prayer Lala, REAL talk. Now I am leaving my desk because I am crying.

My cousin wrote back:

116   *The Final installment of the Kalico Jones Trilogy*

4 Miles to Freedom

Let me say a few things to you. Don't you dare "beat yourself up" for any setback you may have. That is a part of growing. There isn't a person alive (or dead for that matter) who hasn't experienced a setback or two or three or whatever. Not one of us is perfect (no matter how much some would like one to believe). We all have setbacks, whatever they may be. We all have battles to fight, whatever they may be. So you let that go and you walk proud. One day, you'll be able to walk within the NOW and not in the YESTERDAY. It may take some time, but just look forward and stop looking back and believe that you will get there.

Let me tell you something, once you let go of those people draining you, you will be such a different person and you will see life through a brand new set of eyes. And when I pray for you, that's what I pray for. Forget about your "setbacks." I'm not praying for a recovery from your setbacks. Hell we all have setbacks. I'm praying for a complete delivery because your setbacks are a result of deeply rooted and more complex issues. Yes, I do know that much.

It's time for you to completely love Mia Renee. Get to know Mia Renee. Be comfortable with Mia Renee. Be so in love with yourself that you let nobody and I mean nobody (family or otherwise) disrespect you in any way. Love yourself enough to protect yourself. Please. I've felt that pain before and once I learned to love, I mean really love myself, I made a promise to myself that I would never let another soul disrespect me ever again. And I've lived by that ever since. As a result and for the most part, I walk alone and I'm cool with that. I'm good in whatever state I'm in. And sometimes I'm not in such a good state, but I'm good none-the-less. Because in whatever state I'm in, (especially a not so good state) I learn to learn and grow from it and move the heck on. Life is really what you make it Mia. You only have one life. Don't let others dictate to you how your life should be. Most people can't even control their own life so who are they to tell you how you should live yours.

You have so much going for you and you don't even see it. Again I tell you, stop looking behind you and look in front of you. And if you don't like what's in front of you, move it out of your way and if for some reason you can't move it out of your way, then get out of its way. i.e. remove yourself from whatever blocks you...whoever blocks you.

You will be ok and I will talk to you over the phone. But I wanted to send

4 Miles to Freedom

you this email so that you could marinate over what I'm saying and let it really sink in. You are God's "work in progress" Mia, as I am too. Allow yourself to be HIS "work in progress". It's ok...just don't allow yourself to "stay there." Know when to move and know when to move out of the way. It's time to stop blocking your progress.

Love you much cousin and I'll give you a call.

DON'T LOOK BACK

I got up the next morning; got Ivy ready for school and walked by a stack of my books lying on my dining table. "Oh shoot I have to sign a book to Aaron Duncan" I grabbed a book, took out a pen and wrote "Don't look back" and put the book in my bag so that I could mail it out during the day.

And it hit me "DON'T LOOK BACK"

For so many years I have been "Looking back"

Mia was a coke head – using my real name, Mia was a whore, Mia fucked this one...and that one...ALL PAST SHIT...all things from ten to fifteen years ago... nothing current. That's all people from my past life had to talk about.

I guess being a GREAT Mother, having a good job and making a pretty decent writing career for myself wasn't GOSSIP WORTHY...

I changed ALL my telephone numbers.

I just DO NOT want to know.

4 Miles to Freedom

FREE AT LAST... FREE AT LAST... THANK GOD ALMIGHTY... I'M FREE AT LAST

Finally I am FREE and I didn't have to die to get the sort of peace me and my daughter deserve.

Thank you Jesus!

When people see me on the streets, they see something in me ... something they can't quite put their finger on...something that has made me the person I have finally developed to be...sometimes they even say to me, "There's something about you...your honesty, your genuine concern for others and willingness to share...I wonder what made you this way?" and I tell them, "GOD and MY DAUGHTER!"

I've walked through dirt, fire and feces...for what seemed like the longest 4 miles of my life, but I'm grateful for the walk nonetheless. It has made me the person I am. Who is she? SHE'S THE PERSON I ALWAYS WAS.

Panic attacks have subsided. The drinking and late night smokes have slowed, I AM a work in progress and I love my life...oh and I haven't been high in years. Why? Because it just doesn't interest me.

So with having shared that...I will end this book like this...

I AM Mia Renee Williamson. I grew up in a single parent household in the projects of Mt. Vernon, NY with two other siblings. Sexually abused by the very folks who should have protected me (babysitters), I survived. Abandoned continuously for one reason or another until I learned how to...and mastered, the art of abandoning myself.

4 Miles to Freedom

Thank GOD for my daughter, she saved my life. I'm not going to say I haven't slipped up a time or two or three, or four. But I will say, I know how not to wallow in my messes. I get right back up and try it again, knowing I am stronger than yesterday. I walk with my head up high and challenge anyone to say I AM NOT a hero. I AM a hero. I am MY OWN hero. And after trying all the rest, I found comfort in knowing that GOD is with me and has been with me all along. It's a wonderful feeling when you realize that GOD has waited for YOU. You feel special. I'm Renewed in HIM and so I want to just let you know that I...I AM doing JUST FINE!

I'm walking off this stage y'all. I have to go on with my life, I love you and I'll see you guys around.

For more information about me...log onto www.thekalicojonesproject.com to check out what my daughter is up to: www.thedinosaursandsilva.com

And in the words of my father, the Pastor, "Jesus loves you and so do I...bye...bye...bye bye bye!"

4 Miles to Freedom

THANK YOU JESUS!

For allowing me room to see YOU for myself. I thank you for a child who gives me the same feeling I felt when I first looked at her all over again and each time I look at her. She is a person who has her own character and I thank YOU...GOD...for HER. I feel so special about the love YOU have for me. When I think about how YOU waited on me through all my transgressions and craziness, I get chills. I feel BLESSED beyond measure. Thanks to YOU first. Continue to direct my path and continue to use me to be an inspiration to others.

My Parents, Brothers, Sisters, Nieces, Nephews, Cousins, Aunts, Uncles, Grand Parents: Thank you for accepting me for who I am. Allowing me to make mistakes and grow. Now if I could just get one of you to babysit...hahahha. Thanks.

Mike Moore: I love you! And this one is for all the marbles!

Robert Brown aka "My Baby Daddy"...Thank you. Aren't you just so damn proud?

I cannot forget...my ace...Tiph Jackson. (we're like Ike and Tina, but we are thick as thieves and don't apologize).

All my MySpace friends. I love these folks. I have the nicest and most progressive MySpace friends anyone could ask for. We encourage each other and I just love it! I want to tell you guys that I take time out to pray for you and I sincerely wish each of you everything life has to offer: **Tawana, she is the person I call BEFORE and AFTER I do something really stupid** – thanks for hanging in there with me through Yo Nitty...yep I said it. I needed rehab after that experience and NO he is NOT in a book! Sleep – Hold ya head homie, Ant live 129 – Jesus Love you!, LaLa – Y.O.'s favorite girl and someone who I've come to enjoy talking with. This chick makes skinny girls every

4 Miles to Freedom

where jealous, **Yo Nitty aka LOVE FROM AFAR...(this is the person who I talk about needing rehab after) Yo and I go back since he was 17yrs old with Hoop dreams...** *I wont say anything except, I hope you are okay and you know where to find me...no screw that I WILL PUT IT OUT THERE...Yohaun me and you have a serious issue and you know what it is...when you see me, your mouth better say, "Mia, I am sorry" and then we can go from there. Hahaha...I love you Captain!* Nikki Sky, Nik Nak – Nicole Dorns and my cousin Angie who had a baby recently. I know I know...I have to do better with family events and stuff, **Matt Terry who I can have a real conversation with – MINUS this Kalico Jones shhhh – Minus the full face make up and whatever hot lace front I'm rocking this week – Minus the belt bag and shoe habit – Minus what folks think about me and my decisions – HE is my homie 4ever and I wish he would come get the dog I brought him almost two years ago! (inside joke)** Winston aka Daddy Warbucks – I love you and I can't wait to get on that boat! This man has my PERSONAL home number – we rock just like that, Sweet Music – the G String Connection KING, Hollywood of the Hollywood Hang out – who just taught me what an Australian French Kiss was – and not because he did it, but because I asked him for the definition, A.D. – Aaron Duncan "don't look back", Chalah, Moose, Pretty Ricky – Buttah Sopht Ent, Trish aka My Cotton Candy, **Spice Girl – from Brooklyn - MARCIA – who I met personally and I LOVE HER! She's my big Sis,** Headache – NY/NC the one who kept it real about Jay Z, Milz = Mt. Vernon / P.A, My Big Little **Cousin Trouble and his Wife Big Lu and the kids** – P.A / Mt. Vernon, Black ass Inky...I love him – Atl / Mt Vernon, Sexy Chocolate and she knows who she is – Atl / Mt Vernon, Tell big Dee I said Hi and I miss and love her, **Mahogani AKA BIG NEESH – SHERIDAN AVENUE MT. VERNON/ NC..**I love you girl...she IS every hustler's FAVORITE Hustler. **Essence aka Allie McBlack...I love you boo!** Thanks for letting me vent and keeping your mouth shut. ITS HARD BEIND ME...AND SO ITS NICE TO KNOW WHEN ME AND YOU RAP...IM TALKING TO A GROWN WOMAN AND NOT A TAPE RECORDER... You are MY strong people! **Amber Michelle – my MySpace sister and she's a white girl. Amber, I love you babe!** Kenya Renee, my spiritual sister. Thank you for your prayers. I love you and thank you for the scripture about having a wicked tongue. I love you for always pulling me to the side when I mess up. Lisa Bags – You already know,

The Final installment of the Kalico Jones Trilogy

4 Miles to Freedom

Mt. Vernon / Bronx, **I DON'T THINK I MENTIONED THIS BUT HER NAME IS TIFFANY** – Sweet Cooch Brown and those Brooklyn Bombshell Chicks – Star I love your swagger. I love all of them and hopefully by the time you read this...we would have already met. Tiff is adorable and if you come to my MySpace page, she's on the top of my top friends list. I say she's my girl crush. I love her style. Younger ladies...if you want to know how its done...you better take a lesson from these ladies. I'm impressed by the way they move. I love it! **KIMBERLY HATWOOD AND THE KIDDIES AND THAT FINE BROTHER CHARLIE:** I MISS YOU MOMMA, YOU ARE STILL THE STRONGEST WOMAN I KNOW – HEY CHARLIE! HAHAHA (HE'S SAYING THAT'S CRAZY AZZZ MIA AND SHAKING HIS HEAD NO DOUBT. **A.B. Bronx...**NOT the Mt Vernon one, let me be CLEAR – A.B., you and me are tight babe... thanks for believing in me. Who else am I forgetting? Hmmm, Oh **Azizi...THERE'S ONLY ONE...this CHICK still gets the BEST Man title with me whenever I do get married.** J. Garvin and her daughter Saroya who is quickly turning out better than most young women. J you did your THING MISS LADY WITH THAT...Congrats to you and your husband for a Job Well done, both of those young ladies are well on their way! Take a bow Babe.

A very special shout to my 4 mile walk: Here's to you...I walk knowing I owe you nothing. My walk with you is done.

And before you close this book...I want you to pray with me: Ready? Let's do it:

Dear Lord, I thank You for this day, I thank You for my being able to see and to hear this morning. I'm blessed because You area forgiving God and an understanding God.

You have done so much for me and You keep on blessing me. Forgive me this day for everything I have done, said or thought that was not pleasing to you.

I ask now for Your forgiveness. Please keep me safe from all danger and harm.

Help me to start this day with a new attitude and plenty of gratitude.

4 Miles to Freedom

Let me make the best of each and every day to clear my mind so that I can hear from You.

Please broaden my mind that I can accept all things. Let me not whine and whimper over things I have no control over. And give me the best response when I'm pushed beyond my limits.

I know that when I can't pray, You listen to my heart. Continue to use me to do Your will. Continue to bless me that I may be a blessing to others.

Keep me strong that I may help the weak... Keep me uplifted that I may have words of encouragement for others. I pray for those that are lost and can't find their way.

I pray for those that are misjudged and misunderstood. I pray for those who don't know You intimately. I pray for those that will not say this prayer or share it with others, I pray for those that don't believe.

But I thank You that I believe that God changes people and God changes things. I pray for all my sisters and brothers. For each and every family member in their households. I pray for peace, love and joy in their homes; that they are out of debt and all their needs are met.

I pray that every eye that reads this knows there is no problem, circumstance, or situation greater than God. Every battle is in Your hands for You to fight.

I pray that these words be received into the hearts of every eye that sees it in Jesus' name. Amen!

If you prayed this prayer, I believe God is going to do something miraculous in your life and I want you to believe it too!

God Bless ! ! ! ! !

4 Miles to Freedom

Other books by Kalico Jones

EXCERPTS

WHEN GUCCI CAME FIRST

True Tales of a Tramp

And so your journey begins...

Last night, I was out with this guy "Q." He's a fellow PK (preacher's kid) at a bar in New Jersey. After having several drinks "Q" invited me back to his apartment. He said he had access to some good cocaine and since I hadn't seen him in a while I agreed to keep him company.

We walked two blocks from the bar to the apartment he shared with a friend who worked nights. Upon our arrival, "Q" told me that he had to go upstairs to get the "stuff" from a dealer who just happened to live in the building.

He returned 45 minutes later...

4 Miles to Freedom

When "Q" re-entered the room. I immediately asked him how much my portion of the tab was. His response, "Nah Diamond, I got it." Now although my dear friend "Q" had offered to pay for our party favors, I didn't want him to think I owed him a "favor," so I gave him half the money he spent at his neighbor's house, $55.00.

I opened the little plastic baggie and scooped out some of an off-white, really close to yellow substance that was just passed off to me as cocaine and took a hit. Twice up each nostril. My nose froze immediately. I sucked my teeth and said, "There's too much cut on this shit...I can't sniff this crap, shit!" So pissed, having paid $55.00 for garbage, I grabbed a glass, filled it with Bacardi, dropped in two pieces of ice and decided to get drunk instead. But there was one problem, I started feeling high. I thought, "Damn, I hate being high off beat." I sat back on "Q's" bed, smoked a cigarette and waited for my high to come down.

30 minutes later...

My high was gone but my dear friend "Q" was just getting started. He was in the corner of his room (in front of the window, no less), rolling up a dollar bill like a straw. He snorted three lines of cocaine off the top of his dresser. I was flabbergasted and apparently that wasn't enough, because he then poured the little bit of cocaine left in the bag I had in a pipe and lit it!

Oh my goodness, he's a fucking CRACK HEAD! I gotta get the fuck out of here quick. I asked him to walk me back to the bar and he responded with, "Can I have a kiss?"

You should've seen the look on my face, utterly disgusted at this point (I just wasted $55.00 on bullshit, I can't get drunk and now he blows the little bit of high I had with this stupid ass question). "Sorry 'Q' but I don't do anything buzzed." He started laughing and took another hit of his dirty ass pipe. To this day, I have never seen a person suck up smoke the way he did. I know the pipe LOOKED dirty, but was it clogged too? Damn, he needs help. He blew the smoke towards my face and replied in a Jamaican accent, "I respect that."

4 Miles to Freedom

Yeah right...now you know his ass was lying.

"Can we please leave?" I said, as I felt it necessary to ask his ass a SECOND time, to walk me back to the bar. I put on my jacket and told him I was leaving. He said he needed to change his shirt (that took fifteen minutes). He then tried on several suit jackets (another ten minutes) and finally at 1:15am, we were on our way out the door. The bar was closed.

I walked home by myself in the freezing cold, clutching a torn piece of paper with his number on it.

I looked down at his number and thought, "I hope he doesn't expect to hear from me tomorrow." As a matter of fact, I hope he doesn't expect to hear from me ever again, fuckin' CRACK HEAD!

I know, I know, how can I call him a crack head, right?

Listen...I have a weird perception of people who do cocaine. I guess it's because I don't consider myself an addict, and that whole crack pipe, smoking coke thing seems so offensively "fiendish" to me (if that's a word). I feel like this: if you sniff it, that's okay, a rich mans high and as long as you can afford it, you DO NOT HAVE A PROBLEM. Now, if you SMOKE it, you're a fiend, period!

I guess my mindset on this is largely due to the fact that one of the TVs in my home was purchased from a pipe-smoking fiend. It's a sick justification, I know, but as you will see, I've developed many sick justifications over the years.

When I'm not doing cocaine, I have a drink in my hand. I know it's substitution and you better not say shit to me about it, 'cause if you do, I'm gonna say, "At least I'm not getting high!" and I might tell you to go fuck yourself (depending on how many drinks I've had), so mind your fuckin' business!

4 Miles to Freedom

Where are they now?
(The Major Characters from When Gucci Came First)

My mother... When I do signings and speaking engagements I am always asked about the relationship between me and my mother, so I will say this to clear the air...my mother and I are cool peeps. I think we are more "buddies" than mother / daughter sometimes, but she is great at being a Grandmother and me and my daughter love her very much. We've had issues, but they are in the past. I am confident our relationship will continue to grow. **My brothers Joey and Charlie** are the same. ...they both have great jobs and continue to be great fathers to their children and role models to others. **My father** is doing just fine and yes, he is still a pastor in North Carolina. **Hev from Brooklyn** and I are in contact with each other. He owns a club in lower Manhattan and is still keeps a revolving door when it comes to women. **Mr. Moore** and I are still contact. He is in the final stage of his incarceration ...No comment on whether or not we are married. **Mr. Diamond Bracelet** and I are STILL friends, he's a huge part of my past and responsible for most of the good times. I can't go into his whereabouts, but rest assure, I see him a few times a year under the cover of darkness for "federal" reasons. **Mr. Realtor**, still calls me every year on my birthday. **Mr. NBA** is no longer playing professionally. I really don't know how he is and personally I don't care. **Mrs. Mattress Tester from Hempstead a.k.a Nettie** is somewhere in the Bronx. As far as her and I speaking, that will never happen. I'm sure her and homeboy are still in contact, if not, then the fuck was truly NOT worth it. **Monet** and I are sisters for life, I don't see her much, and we don't talk often but when we do, it's a great conversation, and yeah... I still owe her the 100 bucks. **Russ** is married to the woman he was dating when he and I were seeing each other, and GOOD for him! **Mr. GTI** is in jail from my understanding and unfortunately the third party of our "threesome" **Five – Two (really 25)** passed away a few months ago on my birthday. Oh and I never saw **Kelly** again. **Or her father.**

The Final installment of the Kalico Jones Trilogy

*****WHEN GUCCI CAME FIRST, 10 YEARS IN THE GAME...REMIX COMING SOON*********2009

The Final installment of the Kalico Jones Trilogy

4 Miles to Freedom

KJ THREE SIX FIVE (The Diary Vol. 1)

Daily entries taken directly from my site and published, at the advice of my readers.

08/19 - Hello all...today's reflections are a product of family circumstances. I mention the truth shall set you free...so I will say this: What good is keeping "the peace" when the peace is phony? It's your place to demand respect from others and family is no exception. When difficulties arise, get your point across and don't waive your feelings for the sake of keeping peace. You'll only harbor resentment. -kJ

The Final installment of the Kalico Jones Trilogy

4 Miles to Freedom

08/31 -Or what I like to call, "The Final Day of Summer" School shopping, looking for a new place to live - possibly a relocation, and completing my second book. I'm tired, I've got some things going on and I just deleted myself from the long list of Authors groups I belonged to. No reason to explain, just I feel at this time I do not need to be part of a clique to advance in publishing. I feel as though the streets are my reviewers, so no thanks on that. I'm not trying to be funny, I don't think I'm better than others...but lets face it. I'm FROM the streets and so that's who I let judge me. Kalico send us 9 copies of your book for review? NO. Kalico we would like to add you to our web page, just let us review your book, and by the way... we need 4 copies. NO thanks. I will continue to let the streets handle my book sales, and reviews, your help is not necessary at this time. Publishing to me is a business! I'm not here to make friends with everyone who comes across my path. I'm just here to make a difference. I'm sure you can understand that. **So today I say, Blaze your OWN trail. Be your OWN judge and don't let anyone dictate your life to you! peace! KJ.**

09/01- Today's topic. When enough is ENOUGH!

You have friends, you have family, you have associates, all out for one thing, Your time. But when do you begin to put a dollar amount = value on YOUR time? When does your time become valuable to you? I have come to the conclusion - just for today, of course - that my time is VALUABLE and therefore should not be wasted. Don't waste my time. You need something, ask, get it and move on. Don't expect me to babysit you. don't expect me to allow you to reach your goals via my time. I've got my own goals. So any time I take out for you is time taken away from me. So please if someone is nice enough to help you, learn whatever it is they are doing for you, so you can do it for yourself. Don't be a time waster. - **KJ.**

09/03-Well today I will be traveling, actually for the next week I am traveling. Going South. Maybe find a home for my family and me. Check out the book stores in the area, been getting a lot of country love re: When Gucci Came First, so you know a sista gots to go around and check in on those who have supported me. Introduce them to the new books - that's right, BOOKS, plural and just relax. Tried to have a conversation with baby daddy this morning, too bad

4 Miles to Freedom

it didn't Go as planned. Ok see this is why ladies WE have got to do "it" for ourselves. WE have to be independent of the b.s. Life is better for you when you treat baby daddy like a business transaction. Damn shame I have to say this, but you know your girl Kal, she's gonna be real...If he ain't going to give your child the love and respect and most Important, TIME...then make sure your child gets the money. **Don't try to force him to do what he should feel in his heart. Always keeping it real, KJ over and OUT!**

9/13 - The day after the weekend it stormed... I can't even tell you guys how this weekend has made me stop and think, "When did Kalico become a punk?" First, my car was Impounded, yes, Impounded and I was given five tickets two of them court appearances, then I had drama with baby daddy You see, unfortunate for him, he didn't enlist what I like to call, **CONSEQUENTIAL THINKING.** It's when you think about the consequences of your actions frame by frame prior to acting on dumb ass Impulses. You have to evaluate how your irrational behavior is going to affect the overall relationships (you and your children, you and the mother of your child, you and the relatives of the mother of your child, your children's relationships with your family, etc). All these things should be taken into consideration, because when they are, you usually don't show your ass. Today is eviction day for those people who have taken up too much of my mental and emotional time. Eviction day for those individuals who feel as though they are going to affect my life in ways that force me to act out of character...to you, the space holders..."YOUR LEASE IS UP!" The flip side to this is they're all going to make me rich in the long run. **So on this day, Monday September 13, I say to my former tenants "Thank you...now pack your shit and go!" Keeping it real as always, your girl Kal**

09/14 - The day after the day after the weekend it stormed... and **I think I'm going to move.** Relocation may just help me sort the givers from the takers and provide the space between us I need to be able to get things in order. Just because you're an author, of which I do not consider myself to be because my books are truth based and not "made up" (to those who read the original When Gucci Came First: true tales of a tramp). So as I was saying, just because you're an author does mean you're Immune to daily drama and believe me ... I've got my share. Although it has been quiet today. Thank Goodness...**Love**

4 Miles to Freedom

you all -KJ over and OUT!

09/16 - Haters. Today I want to talk about haters in the "writing community" why? Authors don't hate on me because I'm trying to do my thing. Don't hate on me because I deleted myself from all of your groups, don't be mad because it APPEARS that I may be selling a book or two...I say this after seeing a post re: my book. Now for all y'all who know me you know I'm going to keep it real...this post was classless. called my book INANE PRATTLE, etc. Now that would have offended me HAD I NOT been selling books, that may have offended me HAD I NOT been doing my thing on so many OTHER levels, but fortunate for ME, I AM NOT a hater. I don't have to diss any of you authors, and why should I? and why would I? I've got all y'all books! I have support many of my peers, many authors' books are in my home and I DIDNT GET THEM FOR FREE! The ONLY book I have that I didn't pay for is by someone named Natalie, all the others...RIGHT OUT OF MY POCKET. I was the ONLY author out at the Harlem Book Fair giving out my books for FREE! I was the only author who can honestly say they went around and showed loved to EVERYONE! And in the midst of me being KJ...Not one of them said, "Oh let me buy a book from you kj." But did that stop my flow? Hell no. Did that make me not want to support you? Hell no! So why diss me? If I don't want to send books to be reviewed, don't take it personal, **I TOLD Y'ALL I WAS WRITING, LIVING AND DREAMING FOR THE STREETS, its NOT** personal. Kalico Jones is a MOVEMENT, WHERE STREET CREDIBILITY MEETS CORPORATE THINKING. I AM THE BRICK LAYER FOR ALLTHOSE LITTLE KIDS COMING UP WHO ARE IN SITUATIONS WHERE THEY FEEL AS THOUGH THEY CANNOT TURN TO ANYONE. I do many charitable events, I give my time, my money and my spirit for the kids, and don't you even THINK FOR ONE MINUTE YOU CAN JUDGE ME! Please. Now I have better things to do for others, and I cant get them done by allowing the B.S. to get in the way of my goals. Y'all be cool out there. KJ over and OUT! Peace

09/27 - The REAL meaning of keeping it real...and today I'm forced to axe yet another person out of my life. But don't cry for

4 Miles to Freedom

me though, its all good. Now let's get to what I've been up to, my daughter being in a fashion show, dance class, karate, a festival, shopping, dinner, etc. and its been non-stop since Friday afternoon. I've been all over with an authors meeting, a book club meeting and just being a mommy. So between my little princess and my own stuff, it's been one heck of a couple of days. Her fashion debut...well you know how that went down...SHE DID HER THING! she was cute and professional, let me tell you, I may be grooming the next T. Banks. And the dance class, she was terrific! Did you expect anything less than perfection? Of course not! lol. I'm a proud mom. And I should be., it's really all good and I can look and say, **"this is because of me" and God has my back and YOURS too! See ya when I see ya...Kali**

4 Miles to Freedom

MAN UNNECESSARY
COMING SOON

For all the men who want to know why some women would rather go through life alone than with you.

Meet Edna.

Lets talk about Edna. A project chick with a lot of gusto. Edna loves to live life fast and free. She has no kids, no job, a body that doesn't quit and great facial features, she's a ghetto superstar! You know the saying, "Travel light, travel far!" and that's exactly how Edna lived her life. Every day she kissed the sun as she entered her apartment from the night before. Every night finding new faces in crowds where only

The Final installment of the Kalico Jones Trilogy

4 Miles to Freedom

real players play.

Until…One day after hanging out at the Waterfront Bar & Grill she decides to get in the car with a man she met earlier that night through a friend.

He raped her.

People around the way blamed it on her, saying she should not have taken a ride with someone she didn't know personally, and that may be true in this case, but is it right to blame the victim?

Edna has since become an active voice in her community, speaking out about rape, and offering counseling to women who find themselves victims of this kind of behavior. As of today I can't give you an update, because unfortunately Edna is too busy to talk due to the high volume of victims she sees on a daily basis.

Man Unnecessary!

Lesson here, "No means NO!"

4 Miles to Freedom

Karen

Loving, caring, Karen. Grew up the eldest of five and because Karen was the oldest, it was her job to watch her brothers and sisters. Karen resented her mother for forcing her to watch her brothers and sisters, as she was a teen and enjoyed doing teen things. Going to the mall, cheerleading practice, etc. but what could her mother do? Karen's father was not around. And when he was, he was too drunk to care for his own children. He couldn't keep a job and the house payments had to be made. Sometimes there was barely enough money for food, but rest assure in the midst of there not being enough money for food, there was always money for wine and beer.

One payday Karen's mother comes home with bags and bags of groceries for Karen and her siblings. The father walks to the kitchen, shuffles through the bags and yells out to Karen's mother, "Where's my beer?"

"There isn't any."

"What do you mean, there isn't any?"

"There wasn't any money left for me to get your beer."

Karen quickly took the kids into the bedroom, she knew there was going to be fight. Her father always hit her mother when she didn't do as he said. She was scared. But Karen vowed this night would be different. She was determined not to let her father beat her mother up tonight. She told her brothers and sisters to stay in their room, gave them the cordless phone and said, "If you hear screaming, call 911, do you understand?" and in unison her siblings said, "Yes." Karen tiptoed into the hall to get a view of her parents. Her father was now standing in front of her mother holding an empty beer bottle and screaming, "There better be some money left to get my fucking beer!" Her mother took a step back and said, "There is no money left, I have no money, the kids need food."

Karen's father grabbed her mother's purse and looked through it throwing papers, her wallet and other contents onto the floor.

4 Miles to Freedom

"Woman you better go out there and get my fucking beer!" He drew his hand back and slapped Karen's mother to the floor, she let out a scream, "But I have no more money."

"Well then you're gonna get it." He took of his belt and began to hit her. Over and over and over again. Just then Karen runs into the kitchen with a large knife and BOOM!

Karen was too late.

Her mother shot him.

It happened so fast, that her brothers and sisters never got the chance to call 911.

Man Unnecessary!

Stop Domestic Violence. Use your voice, not your fists.

The Final installment of the Kalico Jones Trilogy

4 Miles to Freedom

And to you Homeboy I say Thanks!
The second installment of the Kalico Jones trilogy

I can't believe I'm stuck here, in the house, with a baby, while HIS ass is out running the streets. I have no money, no food and I'm all the way in Spring Valley.

I called my friend Monet. She left her job and came right over, handed me $100.00 (of which I haven't paid her back to this date) and proceeded to give me the advice that every woman in my situation gets from that one girlfriend, who even though you are down in the dumps, feels she has to give you in order to **KEEP IT REAL...**

"Girl you need to leave his ass! This shit is crazy, in the house with a newborn and no money, he can't be serious!" she continued... "Where's the food? Where's the pampers?"

That's when it HIT me, my ass needed to put together that FUCK YOU money quick. I had to not only exit, but exit with a kid. Where did this go wrong?

I checked the time; it was 1 O'clock in the afternoon, is he okay? And if he is okay, where is he?

4 Miles to Freedom

The phone rang.

Ring...ring...

"Hello" (it was a famous R&B singer)

"Yo what up Kalico, yo "Wiz" (short for Wisdom), just left my house, he's on his way home, aight?"

I said okay and hung up the phone. I was on fire. How DARE Mr. Famous R&B Singer call my house to tell me that MY MAN was on his way home at 1 O'clock in the afternoon. Where in the hell was he all night? I put the baby in her crib and waited for him to open the door. It's now 2:30pm and homeboy is just walking in the house! He's drunk and shit...looking pitiful, talking about, "I know...I know...I fucked up, I'm sorry...you mad?"

I took a deep breath, no this nigga did not just ask me if I was mad, he must have bumped his fucking head on the way upstairs. I closed my eyes and thought to myself...I should slap his ass but he's so drunk he probably wouldn't feel it. I will be calm...I will not hit him...I will just leave...I will be calm...I will not hit him...I will just leave...I will be calm...I will not hit him...I will just leave.

I looked at him and in a damn near whisper said, "Yes, I am mad, I'm furious, you're a father now, we are a family, this is crazy...I'm leaving!"

4 Miles to Freedom

TWO WEEKS LATER I WAS GONE!

4 Miles to Freedom

Who is MiMi Williamson aka Kalico Jones?

Mimi Williamson is the founder of *The Kalico Jones Project (an online business networking group for African Americans)* and Sole Proprietor of *WildChild Press*, an independent publishing resource for authors who wish to self-publish their works.

She is a resident of East Orange, New Jersey by way of Mt. Vernon, NY where she continues to lend her support. In 2007, *Mimi Williamson* assisted her hometown with it's Mayoral campaign by hosting several online radio interviews with current Mayor Mr. Clinton Young and former Mayor Mr. Ernest Davis, which was one of the closest Mayoral races in Mt. Vernon history, and by far the most controversial.

Her grass roots approach to rally young voters was recognized and applauded by both current Mayor Mr. Clinton Young and former Mayor Mr. Ernest Davis.

As a young lady who grew up in an environment that was abusive. *Mimi Williamson*, made a conscious decision to not only pen her life story under the brand, *"Kalico Jones"* but to actively work to assist young people in their quest to become successes in their own right. She prides herself on her determination to "Beat the odds" by focusing on her education and natural talents.

Although her titles (five books and counting...) are not for audiences under 18, *Mimi Williamson's* life experiences give her added value at

4 Miles to Freedom

what she does. Physically abused, sexually abused, emotionally abused, drugs, being kicked out of school at 16, *Mimi Williamson* appeared to be a statistic.

But despite being told she would never amount to anything, *Mimi Williamson* turned her life around. She set realistic goals for herself and achieved them one by one. At 19 she graduated from Monroe College in New Rochelle, NY and by the time she was 21, she was working at a leading Wall Street firm. She then went on to secure positions within National Geographic Magazine, Deloitte & Touché and WorldCom, all leading companies in their respective fields at the time.

During her "time" in Corporate America, *Mimi Williamson* realized her true passion; to work with "at risk" teens and women / families in transitional stages, and so I introduce to you...*Mimi Williamson* AND *The Kalico Jones project*.

COMMUNITY INITIATIVES UNDER THE KJP:

CROSS OUR T'S

Cross Our Ts was created by Mimi Williamson, who has taken a personal interest in promoting the importance of education, self respect, and health & well being to teens, including HIV/AIDS prevention, through interactive teen friendly seminars.

"Cross Our T's offers teens REAL life solutions in an open dialogue to REAL life issues and concerns."

KJ CARES

A community based organization that believes in grassroots approaches to community challenges. Fund Raising initiatives. Voter registration drives. Food / Clothing drives. A true effort to immobilize the surrounding community leaders / business owners, residents to GIVE BACK!

The KALICO JONES Project

Black2Black Business Networking

The Final installment of the Kalico Jones Trilogy

4 Miles to Freedom

Mission: To provide a networking resource that expands the possibilities of initial ideas, and concepts according to the "each one teach one" methodology for the African American Community.

"By sharing information we allow our efforts to be supported and developed through the experiences and assistance of others."

KJ's KIDS

For Kids, about Kids, KJ loves the kids!

Events / Book Clubs / Scholarships and more!

For speaking engagements please call 973-672-2753

Email: kalicojones@yahoo.com

Website: www.thekalicojonesproject.com

"The Cross Our T's" initiative & The Kalico Jones Project is a wonderful program headed by a person who in all rights is a hero herself."

The Final installment of the Kalico Jones Trilogy

www.ingramcontent.com/pod-product-compliance
Lightning Source LLC
LaVergne TN
LVHW091553060526
838200LV00036B/821